The Basilwade Chronicles

The Basilwade Chronicles

Dawn Knox

Chapeltown Books

British Library Cataloguing in Publication Data
A Record of this Publication is available from the British Library

ISBN 978-1-910542-49-1

This edition published 2019 by Chapeltown Books
Manchester, England

All Chapeltown books are published on paper derived from sustainable resources.

Contents

A Question of Timing 6
In MaryWorld 13
Knit and Natter 22
Mint Pink 32
Sydney Jugg's Book of Grievances 42
"Is There Anybody There?" 52
Going Freelance 62
So App-ealing 72
No Saints at All Saints' 80
A Meal of Biblical Proportions 89
It is Better to Give than to Receive 99
Superhero Worship 108
Playground Justice 119
Politically Correct at Christmas 130
The Life Coach 139
The Hen Night 146
The Stag Do 160
The Perfect Wedding 172
About the Author 197

A Question of Timing

It was all about timing, Derek decided.

Although arguably, it could be said to be all about *time*. And that was a commodity that Derek had very little of.

That wasn't quite true, of course, he had as much time as the next man but there was only a certain amount of it that he was willing to sacrifice in order to find a wife.

So, when he'd seen the advert for speed dating, he'd been rather excited although he'd been less enthusiastic when he realised it didn't refer to dates that were concluded so rapidly he had time to catch the last bus home. It was disappointing to learn exactly what speed dating was but hardly surprising really. After all, how many women would settle for a packet of chips, a quick cuddle and if she was lucky, a kiss?

He knew exactly how many women *wouldn't* settle for that.

From experience.

He'd always offered to pay their bus fare home. But some women were so unreasonable. Fancy expecting him to go *with* them! It just wasn't logical for him to take a woman out, escort her back to her house and then find his way home. It got to be quite pricey too. And don't get him started on the length of time the whole thing would take.

He turned the page of the newspaper and was

about to forget the advert when he had second thoughts. What did he have to lose? After all, if it got too late, he could simply walk out and go home. All before the last bus.

Derek arrived in the church hall half an hour early, as suggested by the information leaflet he'd received after registering. He ran his finger round the inside of his shirt collar. It was too tight, but by the time he'd realised it earlier this evening, there'd been no time to do anything about it. The top button was undone and his tie pushed up as high as his Adam's Apple would allow. It would have to do.

He looked at his check list. *Item one: Mingle and talk to people.* Well, that was easier said than done. Women were either chatting in groups or not making eye contact with him.

Item two: Smile.

He smiled. After several minutes, women who'd failed to meet his gaze, now stepped sideways away from him.

Probably gone to the Ladies, he thought, *probably nerves.* It might be an idea to visit the Gents himself.

When he emerged, one of the women who'd previously avoided eye contact, now couldn't take her eyes off him. He smiled at her. She was obviously checking him out although when her glance flicked up to his smiling face, her expression froze and immediately she looked down. She swallowed; her eyes closing and bulging open with the effort, then walked towards him.

You've still got it, Derek, old chap! He thought. She sidled up and as she leaned confidentially towards him, he noticed she was jabbing the air with her forefinger, pointing at his trouser zip.

"Wardrobe malfunction in the privates," she whispered from behind her other hand, and glided away.

"Derek Carruthers," he said, holding out his hand, "and you are?"

"Lydia Allen." Her eyes flicked down to check his flies.

He sat down quickly and under the table, he probed the zip to ensure it was still firmly in place.

"I hope you don't mind me... You know... pointing out..." she stabbed the air with her finger which was aimed through the table at where she thought his crotch might be.

He squirmed.

"Yes, oh yes, thank you. It could have been embarrassing."

Silence.

Item three: Ask each partner about themselves.

"So, Lydia, tell me about yourself."

"Well, there's not much to tell really..."

"Okay, well I'll tell you about me then."

There was a lot to tell and it was important to get things in chronological order.

Lydia checked her watch. "One minute to go," she said.

"Goodness, nine minutes went fast! And I'd only got up to when I won the interdepartmental darts tournament in 1998. Oh well."

"Don't forget your match card and pencil," she said pushing them towards Derek. "Ten seconds, nine seconds…"

"Well, thank you very much," said Derek, holding out his hand, "and better luck with the next man." He placed a cross next to her name and moved to the adjacent table.

"Derek Carruthers," he said, holding out his hand, "and you are?"

"Susie Patterson, pleased to meet you."

"Likewise. Well, I hope you're a bit more interesting than the last lady. She didn't have much to say for herself. Dull as ditch water."

"Really? Normally you can't shut her up."

"You know her?"

"Lydia's my sister."

"Derek Carruthers," he said, holding out his hand, "and you are?"

"Maisie Ferguson, it's nice to meet you, Derek."

"You too, Maisie. You're not related to… her? Are you?" he asked nodding at Susie.

"No, who's she?"

"Never mind. Well, tell me about yourself."

"Um, where to start?"

"Let me guess what you do for a living."

"O... okay."

"Now, let me see. I bet you have a food-related job. Cook or something like that."

"No. I work in a dry-cleaners. What made you think I worked with food?"

She looked alarmed. "Do I smell of food? Is that it?"

"No, not at all. I can smell something like tuna but I don't think it's you."

"So?"

"Well, you never see a skinny cook, do you?"

"I see." Her shoulders sagged.

"Out of interest, what's your opinion on just having a bag of chips for dinner?"

"I tend to keep away from chips," she said, "they're very fatty."

"Don't tell me you're on a diet!"

"Well yes, as a matter of fact..."

"Oh, you don't need to diet."

"I don't?" She smiled.

"Oh no. I always think once you've reached a critical weight, there's no point dieting. You might as well just give up and enjoy it. Once you're obese, it's too hard to lose those inches, isn't it? Mind you," he said confidentially, "deciding when you've reached that weight is the crucial thing. I'd say I've got about another stone to go..." he grabbed the flab round his waist with both hands and jiggled it, "… and then I might as well give up being careful with what I eat. It'll all be downhill from there but who cares eh? It's compensation for getting old, isn't it? I mean why make your life miserable in your autumn years? Scoff what you like and hang the fat, I say."

"Derek Carruthers," he said, holding out his hand, "and you are?"

"Dottie Regan. Hi, how are you?"

"Well…"

"You don't sound very sure, Derek."

"Well, it's just that all the women I've met so far seem very prickly. I'm beginning to wonder if I shouldn't just give up. I haven't ticked anyone on my match card yet and I'm nearly at the last table. I'm beginning to get desperate."

"I see, well perhaps your expectations are too high. What exactly are you looking for in a lady friend?"

"Hmm, well I suppose someone who's not the size of a Zeppelin like number five, and preferably a woman without a moustache like number seven. I don't think it was totally inappropriate to enquire whether she was one of those transgender people. I mean I'm liberal and I really wouldn't mind, but it's important to know which bits of equipment she or he comes with. Don't you think? It didn't seem too much to ask. Number eight said I looked like a stalker and asked me to stop smiling at her. I ask you! That's item two on the list! It says smile. So, I keep smiling…"

"Perhaps vary it a little," said Dot, surveying him with her head on one side. "Such a fixed smile is actually rather creepy, if you want my opinion. Move your mouth about a bit."

"Like this?"

"Hmm, perhaps not quite so mobile. Think more Cary Grant… and less guppy."

Derek placed a large cross next to Dot's name and stood up.

"Derek Carruthers," he said, holding out his hand, "and you are?"

"Mary Wilson." She checked her watch and stood up. "Nice to meet you, Derek Carruthers, but I'm afraid I'm going to have to go. Sorry."

"That's fine," he said, "I wasn't going to tick you anyway. I'm not partial to ginger-haired women."

"You're not my type either. What a waste of time, eh? I didn't find anyone," said Mary.

"I'm not surprised."

"What d'you mean you're not surprised?"

Derek looked her up and down. "Well, you're not exactly—"

"Sorry, must dash," she said putting her coat on. "I'd love to stay and chat but if I don't hurry, I'll miss the bus."

"Wait for me," said Derek, "I'll walk you to the bus stop."

In MaryWorld

Mary Wilson dragged a comb through her ginger hair and pulled until the curls surrendered, allowing it to reach her shoulders. But when the teeth finally slipped free of the tangles, the hair sprang back to her ears in corkscrew curls. She frowned at her reflection in the mirror. Tight, ginger curls. There was nothing wrong with curly, ginger hair of course. Come the day when she moved to a deserted island and established MaryWorld, curly, ginger hair would be compulsory. It was just unfortunate that at the moment, no one lived in MaryWorld except her. There were lots of facts and truths in MaryWorld that didn't get much credence elsewhere.

Or, as Mary's mother put it, "You're a one off, dear. Completely out of step with the rest of the world. Always been a little madam, haven't you?"

And that wasn't all Mary's mother had to say about her daughter.

Take that morning at breakfast, for example.

"If you don't get a move on and find a husband soon— "

"Yes, I know, Mother, I'll be left on the shelf—"

"On the shelf? You'll be lucky to get as far as the shelf. You'll be packed away in some cupboard somewhere with all the rejected—"

"Yes, thank you, Mother."

"Although…" Mrs. Wilson slid a newspaper

cutting across the breakfast table, "you might rescue things at the eleventh hour. Speed-dating is the new way to meet a man."

"It's hardly the eleventh hour, Mother! I'm forty-two."

"Exactly, I rest my case. Forty-two! I was eighteen when I married."

"Yes, but you didn't even like Dad."

"What's that got to do with the price of fish, eh? At least I wasn't on the shelf at forty-two."

"Neither am I apparently. I'm in the reject cupboard."

"Don't be facetious." Mrs. Wilson tapped the advert… again and again and again.

"Oh, all right!" Mary snatched the clipping from the staccato beat of the yellow fingernail.

And that was how she met Derek Carruthers. Not that she'd liked him at first. She might have given in to her mother over the speed-dating evening but she wasn't going to miss the last bus home because of it. Derek had been her last partner and he hadn't made a promising start, remarking that he disliked ginger-haired women. Well, she hadn't liked the look of him either. He had strands of grey hair combed over his bald head like strings on a strangely shaped musical instrument and a florid complexion that she later discovered was caused by his tie being pushed up to conceal the fact that his shirt collar was open because it was too small.

Sartorially elegant, he was not.

But that was good because Mother would hate his clothes sense and that might be enough to persuade her that Mary should stop seeing him. And then she'd have breathing space until Mother once again remembered Mary wasn't married.

But she was getting ahead of herself. They'd only been on one date – if you could call it that. She *had* called it that when telling Mother about it, although it was unlikely that Derek would have seen it as such. While they'd ridden on the last bus back to Basilwade together after the speed-dating event, he'd mentioned that she'd reminded him he needed mouthwash and that the cheapest place to buy some – should she feel the need – and he thoroughly recommended that she did – was Asco's supermarket. Aware that Mother would be critical if she didn't have any positive news from the speed-dating, Mary announced at breakfast that she was going on a date and had then spent most of the following morning prowling the aisles of Asco's in case Derek should appear. She was just about to give up and go home when he rounded the corner, pushing a trolley.

"I'm just buying mouthwash," she said casually and after that, one thing led to another and they found themselves in the Asco coffee shop.

He'd invited her out for a stroll through Basilwade on Saturday evening and he'd even bought her a bag of chips. Not that she liked chips but she was quite peckish after their walk and it didn't look like Derek was going to take her to dinner.

She was torn. Derek was definitely not the man of her dreams – there *were* no men in her dreams, indeed no men at all in MaryWorld – but in order to keep Mother off her back, she needed to show she was trying.

"… so, if you care to come round on Sunday, for tea, you can meet my mother…"

"Whatever for?"

"Well, I live with her, so if you come round for tea, you're bound to bump into her."

"I see. Well yes, all right then. How long will it take? The Grand Prix is on at half past seven and I never miss it."

"If you leave at five, I'm sure you'll get home in time."

Now, how to introduce Derek to her mother?

'Boyfriend' was a ridiculous term. Derek had not been a boy for a long time. If ever. 'Manfriend' sounded just as silly. She'd overheard her next-door neighbour's teenage daughter at the bus stop the other day talking about her latest, and she'd used a term… now what was it? She must try to remember. It would be good to sound modern but casual. Slightly committed but not too committed. Yes, she definitely had to establish a word to describe Derek before Mother started calling him her *intended* or *fiancé*.

Mary had anticipated that Derek would arrive early, so the table was laid and they were already seated when her mother came into the dining room.

"Derek Carruthers," said Derek standing up and holding out his hand, "and you must be Mrs. Wilson."

"How d'you do, Derek…" She fixed him with a steely stare. "So, you're the man on benefits."

"I don't believe so," said Derek sitting down and taking the large slice of fruitcake that Mary offered him.

"Oh Mother! Derek isn't *on* benefits."

"But you said—"

"I said he was my friend *with* benefits."

Derek choked, spraying Mrs. Wilson with fruitcake crumbs.

"Well, what on earth does that mean? Benefits? What sort of benefits?" Mrs. Wilson asked, flicking fruit off the front of her blouse.

"Oh, Mother! Honestly, you're so behind the times."

"That's as may be," said Mrs. Wilson.

A piece of cake had gone down the wrong way and Derek was finding it difficult to breathe. Mary slapped him hard in the middle of his back and with his airway free at last, he clawed at his collar, gasping for air.

"Well, I'm going to take Twinkle for a walk, so, I'll leave you to it," said Mrs. Wilson picking a half-chewed currant off her sleeve and dropping it on the plate. Whistling for Twinkle, she rose and left.

"*Leave us to it?* You mean?... What, *here?*" asked Derek. "*Now?*"

"Well, yes. Now's as good a time as any." Mary looked at the enormous cake she'd made that morning. Surely, he wasn't going to leave immediately? Mother was enough to intimidate anyone but if he was gone before she got back, it would be obvious the date hadn't gone well. "Mother will be out for a while. It takes her about twenty minutes to go round the block," she added, hoping he'd stay at least until she returned.

"Twenty minutes! Look, I'm all for saving time and I know I said I wanted to be gone by five o'clock but this has all been a bit of a shock. I'm sure once I get going it won't take long but I might need a few minutes to summon my... well, to prepare myself... to build myself up, as it were..."

"What for?"

"Well... *it.* You know... *the benefits.*"

Mary didn't know. The only benefit she required was that Derek remained in her life long enough to stop Mother criticising, and then to give her time to realise that her daughter was better off without him.

"More tea? Cake?" she asked weakly.

"Have we got time for tea and cake as well as... it?"

"Well, it's up to you. How much time have you got to spare?"

He checked his watch. "Hmm. I'm not sure. Only eighteen minutes left until your mother gets back. Suppose she returns before we've finished?"

"Oh, don't worry about her," said Mary looking at the large slab of cake. They definitely wouldn't finish *that* before she got back. "Look, forget Mother. I know she can be critical but—"

"*Critical?* Critical of what? You're making it sound like she's going to give us marks out of ten!" Derek mopped his forehead.

"Well, she can be a bit demanding but—"

"You haven't got a shot of whisky, have you? Or two? I think I need help."

"Mornin'." Florrie Fanshawe from next door rushed to her doorstep when she saw Mary walking down the garden path with Twinkle. "That was a lot of commotion in your house yesterday afternoon…"

"Yes." Mary sighed. "Men are such strange creatures…"

"Oooh, I know. The late Mr. Fanshawe was very peculiar. Who was that man your mum had in a half-nelson? I almost felt sorry for him. Mind you, when she tipped him over the garden gate, he was off like a shot. Never seen anyone so bulky move so fast."

"Yes, he definitely was a fast mover. Very fast indeed," said Mary through clenched teeth.

"What! You mean? No! Don't tell me he tried it on?"

Mary nodded.

"With *you?"* Florrie asked incredulously.

"Yes! With *me!* I was just passing him another slice of fruitcake when he lunged."

"Oooh I say. The beast! *Lunged*, you say?"

"Yes, *lunged!* His hands were everywhere. Even places I didn't know I had. If mother hadn't come back when she did who knows what might have happened? Mind you in a way it's mother's fault I was in that predicament. She was the one who convinced me to go speed-dating!"

"O-oh!" said Florrie with sympathy. "Well, why don't you try online dating? That's the way people meet up nowadays."

"I'm not very confident with computers. I can just about manage to look up the bus timetable but I wouldn't know how to do online dating."

Mary looked thoughtful. "Err, you don't think your Amy could help me, do you? She seems to be an Internet expert, she's always got that phone inches from her nose."

"Well, I could ask her but I don't think she knows anything about dating apps."

"Yes, I think she does. I was standing behind her at the bus stop the other day and she was telling her friend about someone she'd met online."

"My Amy? No, I think you're mistaken. She's only sixteen. I'd know if she had a boyfriend."

"Well, he wasn't exactly a boyfriend. She said he was her friend with benefits... Florrie? Are you all right? You seem rather overwrought..."

Florrie was stomping up the path to the house. "Ameeee! You get yourself down here right now my girl! You've got some explaining to do!"

Despite Twinkle trying to drag her out for a walk, Mary crept back into the house. Every time she'd mentioned the phrase 'friend with benefits', the world had gone mad. She sat down at the computer and logged on.

Colour drained from her face as she read the definition. So, it was a euphemism for two people who were simply together so they could... Blood rushed back into her face, making her cheeks throb with embarrassment.

Come the day when she moved to a deserted island and established MaryWorld, dating would be banned, men would be banned, mothers would be banned and benefits of any description would be banned.

And euphemisms would be banned too.

Knit and Natter

"D'you think that'll be enough?" Florrie Fanshawe asked, stabbing the air with a bony finger as she counted each of the plastic chairs she'd arranged around the community hall table.

"Mm hmm, six should be enough," Harriet replied. "Peggy's still got the 'flu, Doris is in Brighton and as for poor Gladys…" She crossed herself.

"Oh, yes, Gladys, poor thing. Is she still…?

"Mm hmm."

"Oh dear."

Florrie wiped her skeletal finger across the top of the table and inspected it. "Just look at this!" she held out the evidence. "Filth!" Clicking open the clasp on her handbag, she pulled out a pack of wipes and scrubbed at the pitted, wooden surface of the table. Once satisfied, she fished in her handbag again and produced a spray of air freshener from which she let out several frenzied blasts. A fragrant, lemon scent struggled bravely with the musty, fusty air in the community hall but was soon vanquished.

"What's the target now?" Harriet asked as Florrie took a pile of knitted squares from a large carrier bag and placed them in the middle of the table.

"Well, we were aiming for ten blankets but we seem to have got through the first four quite quickly, so I'd like to suggest we increase it to a dozen. What d'you think?"

"Mm hmm. The people at the dog's home are always appealing for extra blankets, so I'd say yes. It looks like Knit and Natter is a great success. Perhaps we ought to pay for the hall for a further three months."

"Yes, I think you're right."

When everyone had arrived, Florrie took a notebook from her capacious handbag and listed everyone's name. "Harriet Pettara, Edna Harbottle, Mary Wilson, Rita Gupta, Sebastian Milligrew…" she turned to the new lady, "and you are?"

"Bella Carrossetti, two R's, two S's and two T's."

"Rrsstt?" asked Florrie reading what she'd written.

"Well, I expected you to work out all the other letters yourself." Bella shook her head in disbelief and the bun on top of her head wobbled precariously. "Here," she said taking a handful of business cards from her pocket with a perfectly manicured hand and distributed one in front of each person at the table.

"Bella's Beauty Box," she said proudly. "I'm the proprietor. Beauty in Basilwade or Wherever You Are," she added. "Ten percent off on presentation of this card."

"Oh my!" she said as Rita reached out to take the card that had been placed in front of her. "Don't worry, there's nothing to be ashamed of," she added as Rita snatched her hand away. "False nails would be perfect for you. There's not much you can do with nails that shape or in that state but I'll be able to make them look reasonable. Just give me a ring and ask for a Bella's Special Manicure."

Rita stared at the card as if willing it to glide towards her without having to expose her hands again.

"And don't think that gentlemen aren't welcome, I have lots of male customers. It's really quite manly now to have manicures," Bella said to Sebastian who thrust his hands in his pockets and shrank behind Edna.

"Or facials," Bella added.

He's rather shy, mouthed Edna.

"He's what?" Bella asked, craning her neck to get a better look at Sebastian who checked his watch, rose apologetically, his face crimson. He mumbled something and rushed out.

Everyone looked accusingly at Bella.

"Oh my!" she said. "He forgot his card. 'Scuse me a moment, while I chase after him—"

"No!" said the Knit and Natter ladies in unison.

Bella sat down and patted her topknot. "I'll give it to him next week."

"Now, if we could get on," Florrie said, glancing sideways at Bella, nostrils flared and eyebrows drawn together. "Well, ladies, we've almost finished blanket number five. Just three more squares needed. We've had suggestions for a colour scheme for number six. Mary would like blue and red—"

There was a sharp intake of breath from Bella.

"Oh, no! Oh my, no! Red and blue will never do," she said in a sing-song voice.

Harriet, the peace-keeper, replaced the blue wool that Florrie had laid next to the red one with a green ball.

Bella tutted.

"Red and blue will never do. Red and green should never be seen," Bella said.

Florrie turned to Bella and fixed her with the look that even Amy, her teenage daughter, with all the insouciance of youth, recognised as a tipping point before a cataclysmic eruption. Florrie was halfway through the inhalation that would launch the explosion when Bella leapt up.

"Stop right there! Freeze!" said Bella.

Florrie stopped and froze.

Bella pulled a pair of tweezers from her pocket and grabbed Florrie by the chin.

"There!" she said triumphantly as she applied the tweezers to Florrie's jaw and plucked.

"I've never seen such a large whisker on a woman before," she said holding the hair still trapped between the jaws of the tweezers so that all the ladies could admire it.

"Would you like me to dab that with witch hazel? I swear by the stuff," she asked Florrie who cradled her chin as if she'd been punched. Florrie shook her head, eyes wide with shock.

The other ladies surreptitiously probed their faces with exploratory fingers, all eyes on Bella.

"Oh my!" said Bella whose gaze had alighted on Harriet. She sprang to her feet. "Such tension!" Bella rolled her sleeves up and reached out as if to play the piano. Harriet gulped and her eyes swivelled in their sockets as she tried to see behind her without moving her head which was now clamped in Bella's vice-like grip. With elbows raised, she began to knead the muscles in Harriet's neck and shoulders.

"Oh my! I've never felt such locked muscles. How on earth d'you move your head?" Harriet's eyes were watering as Bella squeezed and pulled, then performed some chopping actions with the edge of her hand.

"*HELP!*" mouthed Harriet. But no one dared move.

"Better?" Bella asked silkily, poking her head over Harriet's shoulder.

Harriet nodded.

She was beyond speech.

"Goodness me," said Edna, checking her watch, "is that the time? I really should be going." So far, she and Mary had been the only ones to escape Bella's scrutiny.

"So soon?" said Florrie, whose tone dripped acid. She might just as easily have said, 'Sit down! If we've had to put up with these indignities, don't think you're going to get away with it!"

Edna went into the kitchen with a toss of her head and returned a few minutes later with a tray of mugs and a plate of biscuits.

"Tsk," said Bella wagging her finger at Edna. "What crosses the lips ends up on the hips." She half-rose to peer over the top of the table at Edna's ample hips, then moved the plate out of her reach. "I've got the perfect diet regime." She splayed thumb and little finger as if representing a telephone receiver and mouthed, "*Phone me.*"

"Well, if we can proceed," said Florrie with a quick glance to her left to check on Bella.

"So, what do we do?" asked Bella.

"The clue's in the name!" snapped the usually peaceful Harriet, picking up her knitting needles. She aimed the points at Bella.

"Indeed," said Florrie, "we knit. We natter. We make squares which we sew into blankets for the local dog's home."

She passed Bella needles and a ball of blue wool. The next blanket *would* be red and blue as Mary had requested. She rubbed the tiny irritated area where until a few minutes ago she'd unknowingly harboured a whisker. Yes, red and blue would definitely do. She'd make sure of that!

"Oh my!" said Bella.

Everyone went rigid, heads moving like meerkats.

"You're knitting a triangle. I thought you said squares?"

Harriet dropped three stitches as she turned, her needles pointing towards Bella and eyed her warily. "We knit from corner to corner."

"But I don't know how to do that."

"Oh dear," said Florrie, keeping her chin tucked down, "well, I don't have the pattern on me," she said pushing her bag containing the patterns further under the table with her foot. "And we're all decreasing, so no one can demonstrate how to do it. Oh dear."

Five pairs of needles clickety clacked faster and faster, as if out of control.

"I know," said Florrie, "I'll bring the pattern next week. So, rather than waste your precious time now…" She stood ready to escort Bella out, needles still moving so fast they were a blur.

But Florrie's hint was obviously too subtle for the beautician. She slid her chair closer to Harriet who swung round, needles aimed.

"Umm," said Rita who was knitting with her hands under the table, "you could always drop into the dog's home. They've got several of the blankets we've made and there are lots of volunteers there who'd probably love some beauty tips… and your card, of course."

Five Knitter Natterers collectively held their breath.

"Excellent idea," said Bella, patting her topknot and then powdering her nose. She smiled benevolently at the ladies. "Well, no time like the present," she said and rose to go.

"Mm hmm," said Harriet, still holding her breath.

Florrie was the first to breathe out. "Has she gone?"

The high-speed knitting ceased.

"Mm hmm," said Harriet, gasping.

Florrie took out her lemon-scented air freshener and gave two prolonged blasts in the direction of the door. It was hard to tell if she was attempting to annihilate the beautician's lingering floral scent or whether she was imagining she was firing at Bella herself.

"Thank goodness she's gone," said Mary.

"I don't know why you're so pleased, Mary, you're the only one who escaped attention."

Mary's bottom lip trembled. "Not exactly."

"Well, she didn't offer you any 'helpful tips', did she?"

"No but I got plenty of attention. I kept feeling her eyes on me. She was looking at me as if I was beyond hope…"

"I think you're being a bit sensitive, dear," said Rita, her hands curled so her nails were hidden in her palms. "There's nothing wrong with curly, ginger hair. Honestly."

"Nor so many freckles," said Florrie.

"And your face is pleasant being round. It wouldn't suit you to lose much weight," added Edna eyeing the biscuits.

Mary's bottom lip trembled even more.

"Just as well Gladys wasn't here," said Rita.

"Oh yes, poor Gladys. Well, at least she was saved the indignity of an encounter with Miss Basilwade. Although…"

"I know," said Harriet crossing herself. "I think I'd rather an encounter with Miss Basilwade than go through what poor Gladys has been through. Although I still can't work out exactly what happened."

"Me neither. I can't understand where the baked beans came into it."

"No, nor that rabid badger."

"Badger? I thought it was her lodger."

"Was her lodger rabid?"

"I don't know. Someone told me it was a wildebeest."

"Hmm, I'd heard it was a wild beast?"

"Well, one thing's for sure, we won't be seeing Gladys back here for some time."

"If ever…"

The ladies sat silently with their thoughts for a while.

"Suppose Miss Basilwade comes next week?" asked Edna eventually, "she might bring wax or… lasers…"

"Suppose she comes next week, to what?" asked Florrie.

"Knit and Natter, of course!"

"No, she won't be able to, because it's cancelled."

"Since when?"

"Since now."

"Oh, that's a shame. Surely we're not going to let some botoxed bimbo break up our group?"

"Absolutely not," said Florrie. "Next week a new group will meet at my house and it will be called… umm… 'Blankets and Blarney' or 'Squares and Squawk' and the membership is firmly closed."

Mint Pink

Edna Harbottle liked to do her bit for charity. And since the main raffle prize was an enormous hamper, she bought ten tickets. The odds were that she would win something – and she did. Sadly, not the coveted hamper but a complimentary voucher for a home manicure. She'd never been one for fussing about her nails but she thought it might be nice to have a bit of pampering – it would relieve the boredom – and quite frankly, the loneliness that Edna felt during the week while her husband, Roland, was at work. He was a bank manager in Basilwade and took his job very seriously. In two years' time, he'd retire and she wondered how she'd cope with him under her feet for the rest of their lives although if the weekends were any indication of what her future might hold, he'd only be under her feet if she happened to be standing on his favourite armchair. Roland spent Saturdays and Sundays fast asleep in front of the television. After a few weeks of retirement, he'd probably have taken root in that chair. She would still be lonely – the only difference was that she'd have to be quiet about it so as not to wake him up. Yes, a beauty treatment was exactly what she needed to take her mind off the emptiness in her house and the emptiness of her future.

On the eagerly-anticipated day, Edna hovered by the front window, watching for the beautician.

"I don't believe it!" she said when a young woman arrived at her gate.

Edna didn't often swear but it seemed appropriate.

Ducking down out of sight also seemed a good idea.

The doorbell rang insistently and Edna had the feeling the young woman wouldn't go away until someone responded. With a sigh, she stood up and gritted her teeth. On the doorstep, was Bella Carrossetti, the young woman with the top-knot who'd insulted so many members of the Knit and Natter club that it had changed venue, meeting day and name.

'Blankets and Blarney' now took place in Florrie Fanshawe's house on Friday morning which meant Edna had to wait the whole week for some excitement.

"Bella's Beauty Box. Beauty in Basilwade or Wherever You Are," Bella said in a sing-song voice, gripping a box with one hand and patting her top-knot with the other.

No, it was too late to cancel.

"Come in," said Edna.

"Oh my," said Bella "what a… well… period room. I mean, how very Victorian."

Edna looked round her living room.

Victorian? Well, it was a bit shabby, that was for sure. She'd begged Roland to redecorate but he was always too tired. Or asleep.

But Victorian?

"It's so very… brown. Not that there's anything wrong with brown… or Victorian, of course," said Bella when she saw Edna's mouth opening and closing. No sound was coming out but even Bella could tell that as soon as Edna recovered her composure, the sounds she emitted, would be indignant.

"Well, shall we begin?" asked Bella brightly. "By the way, you look very familiar, have I done your nails before?"

She peered at Edna's fingers which were gripping the back of Roland's armchair. "No, I can't have," Bella said. "I wouldn't have let them get in that state."

After an unpromising start, Edna found the whole manicure experience quite pleasant. Bella chatted about men, nails, more men and more nails and Edna let it wash over her. It was nice to hear another voice in her living room – even if what it was saying wasn't worth listening to.

"So, what d'you think?" asked Bella. "This one or this?" She put two bottles of nail varnish on the table – one pillar box red and one bright orange.

"Haven't you got anything a bit paler?"

"This?" Bella replaced them with a pretty, shell-pink bottle.

"Oh, yes, that's perfect."

Bella held the bottle up and glanced round the

room. "You know, it would be a really good colour in here. With matching curtains and cushions."

Yes," said Edna, "you're right but unfortunately, my husband doesn't have much idea about decorating."

"Oh my! You don't need to worry about that. I've just the person who could do it! My uncle's a decorator and he's between jobs at the moment. I'll send him round later today."

"Oh, no! Thank you but—"

"It's no trouble. I'll text him now," Bella said her thumbs a blur over her mobile phone. "There. He'll be round in an hour."

Edna sighed. Roland wouldn't allow it. On the other hand, he couldn't do much about it once it'd been started. And, it wouldn't hurt to meet Bella's uncle. It would fill the afternoon.

"How d'you do, Missus?" A large man held out a hand that resembled a pack of sausages. He had an enormous stomach that bulged out at the front, straining his overalls. "My niece Bella, said you was looking for a decorator. And here I am," he announced proudly sticking out his stomach even further. "Here's my card."

"A Jugg?" she read.

"Yep, that's right. That's me. Anthony Jugg. But my friends call me Toby. At your service, Missus."

And somehow, during that short exchange, Edna found herself showing him into the living room.

"Hoh, yes! I see what Bella meant. This is definitely in need of a makeover. And I'm just the man to do it. I'll start tomorrow."

"Don't we need to discuss prices and things?" asked Edna quickly.

"Hoh no! I'm really reasonable. Tell you what. Gimme a ton and I'll go and buy the paint and paper now."

"A ton? A ton of what?"

"Hoh, bless you Missus! A ton, a hundred quid."

"I don't think so," said Edna sharply, "and anyway, you don't know what colour I want, nor what paper."

"Hoh, it'll be Alan Glupta for the walls. And for a colour… I'm thinking… hmm…" he splayed his hand, palm down on his chest like an artist, as he gazed about. "Yup, I have it. Mint pink."

"Isn't mint usually green?"

"Not when it's pink, Missus, not when it's pink. Here," he said pulling a grimy piece of paper from his pocket and stabbing at one of the coloured splodges with a sausage-finger, "this one."

It was very similar to the shell-pink varnish on her nails.

"It doesn't say Mint Pink," she remarked. "In fact, none of the colours are labelled."

"I knows them colours off by heart. Now, if you can't manage a ton, a pony'll do and I'll rush down to the suppliers before they close."

"A pony?"

"Hoh, Missus!" he said. "You crack me up. A pony, you know, twenty-five quid."

"No," said Edna firmly, "I'll pay you when you've finished and not a minute before. That is, if I engage you at all."

"Hoh, you drive a 'ard bargain, Missus, and no mistake! Right, make it a tenner and I'll be back in a jiffy."

And for some reason that Edna couldn't later justify, she handed over ten pounds.

"Put the kettle on," he said as he swept out of the living room, "leave the teabag in. Milk and two sugars. And I wouldn't say no to a Custard Cream."

By the time Roland put his key in the lock that night, Edna had cleaned most of the mess. Of course, there was no hiding the half-wallpapered walls but she'd managed to wash much of the wallpaper paste off the carpet. Tins of paint stood piled high behind the sofa.

"Why did you buy so much?" she'd asked Toby when he'd returned earlier.

"It's better than not having enough," he said.

"And how did you get so many for ten pounds?"

Toby tapped the side of his nose and winked.

"And how d'you know what colour they are?" Edna asked, noting that the tins were completely unmarked.

"You get a nose for it," he'd said.

"You can smell the colours?" she'd asked incredulously.

Toby had vaguely waved a hand, and set about opening one of them with a screwdriver.

It was grey.

By the fourth tin, she realised why they'd been so cheap. "So, you got this job lot of paint because you didn't know what colour they were? How d'you know any of them are the right shade?"

"Trust me, it'll be all right. Now, how about another cuppa?"

The afternoon had been quite amusing. Toby's clumsiness increased with the number of jokes and stories he told. Well, she'd simply have to change the carpet once the decorating was finished. A leaky tin had resulted in a puddle of blue paint appearing from under the sofa, like a wave on a beach. It had only stopped when it encountered the rug.

But when Roland returned from work, he was less bothered with the mess and more with the paint fumes.

"It's no good," he gasped, clutching his throat, "I can't sit in here. I'm going into the garden."

Edna had expected him to shout or complain or even sulk, so she was rather taken aback when she saw him in the middle of the lawn in a deckchair. He never sat in the garden.

He hated the garden. It was alien territory.

Edna spent the rest of the evening scraping blue

paint off the carpet and washing out more wallpaper paste. By the time she'd finished, the beautiful summer sunset had faded and stars were beginning to twinkle in the night sky. Thankfully, the oppressive heat of the day was replaced by a brisk evening breeze which helped to dissipate the fumes. It was completely dark when Roland came in and went straight to bed.

Toby arrived the following day with his apprentice, Shane, who obviously had more idea than his boss about wallpapering. Edna could hardly boil the kettle fast enough to keep the two men supplied with tea.

While Shane worked, Toby offered advice and told stories.

"Have you heard the one about…?" he asked, repeatedly.

Edna couldn't remember when she'd enjoyed herself more.

"So, you'll be finished tomorrow, Toby?" she asked with disappointment.

"Yup! Work fast, work tidy. That's my motto."

Shane's eyes rolled upwards and nearly disappeared into his eye sockets.

Edna was thrilled with the redecoration. She'd bought new curtains and cushions and the carpet would be fitted on Monday. The days had been hot and still and the paint fumes hung heavily in the living room although thankfully, each evening, a fresh breeze had cleared the room. Nevertheless, when Roland returned from work, he sat outside in the deckchair, first watching the sunset fade and then the stars appear.

Edna felt guilty about forcing him out of the house after a day's work. Should she buy a fan to blow the remaining fumes out of the house even though she could no longer smell them?

No, she decided. Enough was enough. He was being completely childish. Edna marched into the garden.

"Roland, I—"

"Shh!" he said. "Listen!"

She listened.

"What?" she whispered.

"It's the stars. They're tinkling! Isn't it magical? I can't believe I never heard them before…"

He's flipped, thought Edna, the paint fumes have pickled his brain.

"Tinkling?" she finally managed.

"Yes, listen. Can't you hear them?"

"Umm… How about a nice cup of tea?"

"That would be lovely. I'll get another deckchair and we can listen to the stars together."

"Umm… yes, all right."

The fresh evening breeze sprang up and wafted the scent of the honeysuckle into the kitchen after her. And then she realised. Each evening, when the wind began to blow, it agitated the next-door neighbour's new wind chimes.

Did Roland really believe the stars were tinkling? Or was he just being poetic? He'd never been poetic before. But then, he'd once thought sparrows turned into robins in the winter, and that wasps were rogue bees, so anything was possible. But who cared? It'd be lovely to sit in the garden together and listen to the stars. And tomorrow, she'd contact Toby. The dining room could definitely do with a makeover.

Sydney Jugg's Book of Grievances

Sydney Jugg was a man who bore a grudge. Actually, he bore many. Ever since he'd been a small boy, he remembered his mother telling him to 'stop bearing a grudge'. At first, he wasn't sure what a grudge was and Ma's explanation when he'd enquired, hadn't really enlightened him.

"Don't be so cheeky!" she said and swatted him round the head.

Over the years, he'd worked out that *bearing a grudge* was a justifiable reaction to the injustices that life threw at him.

And there were many. For example, his brother, Toby, could charm and beguile anyone. His decorating firm was successful despite Toby's lack of practical skills. And women! Toby's face could best be described as *unfortunate*, and his body was shaped like a barrel. But women were attracted to his ridiculous patter in a way they'd never been to anything Sydney had to say.

And as for business acumen, Toby had none. Sydney, on the other hand, thought up so many business ideas his head spun, but none so far had amounted to anything.

However, this time, he had the King of Ideas. Now all he needed was a rather large bank loan.

He arrived at Bboyds Bank ten minutes before his

appointment with Mr. Harbottle, dressed in his best suit and shiny shoes.

"Mr. Harbottle won't be long. Would you like coffee?" the personal assistant asked. But before he could reply, the bank manager appeared at the door. His shoulders sagged when he saw Sydney.

"Ah, Mr Jugg, isn't it? Please come in."

Roland Harbottle steepled his fingers and resting his chin on the tips, he surveyed Sydney who was sitting on the edge of his chair on the other side of the desk.

"Another *King of Ideas,* Mr Jugg?" Roland asked.

"Yes, but I think you're going to like this one. It can't fail."

"Hmmm. Well, it'll have to be better than the edible chopsticks. Or the magnetic dentures."

"Yes, this one is guaranteed to succeed."

Roland sighed. "Well?"

"You know how everyone loves the smell of bacon..."

"Vegetarians and Vegans probably don't. But I agree it's a popular smell."

"I'd like to develop a men's toiletries range..."

"Please tell me you're not proposing an aftershave smelling of bacon!"

"Well..."

"I really don't think so. Have you done any market research?"

"No, I use common sense. People like the smell of bacon. It's bound to work."

Roland pressed the button on his intercom, "Milly!"

"Yes, Sir," said the tinny voice through the intercom.

"Milly, if you could pick an aftershave for a man to wear, would you pick one that smelled of sandalwood… or perhaps, bacon?"

"*Bacon?*" said the tinny voice. "Sorry, Sir, I thought you said *bacon!*" Peals of laughter could be heard through the intercom.

"I rest my case," said Roland showing the palms of his hands in a gesture of resignation. "Milly has spoken… Now, Mr Jugg, if I were you, I'd forget your get-rich schemes and concentrate on your plumbing business. Your brother's just done an excellent job redecorating my house. You're a perfectly good plumber. Isn't that enough?"

The bank manager got to his feet and held out his hand.

Sydney's interview was over. But before he could leave, Milly poked her head round the door. "Oh, Mr Harbottle, while you've got Mr Jugg here, the radiator in the ladies' toilet is leaking. I wonder if he could fix it."

Sydney stomped out to his van to get his overalls and tools.

What did the bank manager know? Or silly Milly? He wouldn't give up. He'd try elsewhere.

As he worked, he committed the conversation he'd

had with Mr Harbottle to memory so that when he got home, he could record it in his Book of Grievances. The bank manager had turned down several requests for loans and consequently, he had a whole page to himself in Sydney's Book of Grievances. This further insult would be added. Keeping a record each evening assured that no slight, however small, was forgotten. Milly would be added as well. And in the meantime, Sydney thought as he whacked the radiator valve with a wrench, he'd charge the bank an arm and a leg for this job. The valve parted company with the radiator, allowing a spout of rusty water to gush over his shiny shoes.

Sydney wanted more from life than scraping a living tinkering with toilets and taps. He not only *wanted* more, he *deserved* more.

But how?

Yet again, he'd been compared to his brother, Toby, and been found wanting. As he walked past Mr Harbottle's office, he noticed a poster on the notice board. A young couple posed with dumbbells raised as if they weighed nothing, well-defined muscles beneath shiny, tanned skin and their smiles revealing gleaming teeth.

Be The You, You Always Wanted To Be
Muscle Bounders Gym
Book your first session now!

Sydney had once been quite fit. Fitter than Toby, anyway. And a toned body would give him confidence. Yes, he'd sign up with a personal trainer for a month at Muscle Bounders Gym.

"I am Vilya Chekarova," said the personal trainer in a heavy accent. She towered over him, bulging muscles straining her Lycra top and leggings and she shook Sydney's hand, almost wringing it from his wrist. "You must be Syderney."

"Err, it's Sydney."

"That is vot I said… Syderney."

Sydney dared not disagree.

"Now, let us see vot you are made of, Syderney."

Sydney showed her what he was made of.

"Hmm, ve have a lot of vork to do, eh, Syderney?"

As he limped out of Muscle Bounders Gym an hour later, she called after him, "Do not vorry, Syderney, I vill turn you into a man of steel."

His muscles screamed as he gingerly climbed into his van, eased into the driver's seat and slowly drove home. He was too exhausted to make more than a cup of tea and certainly too tired to write in his Book of Grievances. But tomorrow Vilya Chekarova, Mistress of Sadism, would also have her own page along with Roland Harbottle and Silly Milly. And he would cancel his next training session.

The following morning, he ate his breakfast standing up, his joints having locked rigidly overnight. Ahead of him was a full day, plumbing in a bath in a rather small bathroom, and if he was finding it hard to bend down now, how was he going to squeeze himself into whatever shape was necessary to get to the waste and pipes?

He phoned the gym before he left for work.

"Hello, Muscle Bounders Gym, Betty speaking. How can I help you?"

He explained he wouldn't be able to make his next training session because of work pressure.

"I'm sorry you can't make it, Mr Jugg! Never mind, I'll tell Vilya and she can bring round a few weights to your house and do your training session in your home—"

"No!"

"Oh, don't worry, it's no problem. Vilya's used to it. You'd be surprised how often this happens. Have I got your address? Oh yes, here it is. Well, I'll tell Vilya to be there at seven. How will that be? Goodbye now! Have a good day!"

He thumped his mug down on the table, groaning at the pain that radiated throughout his body. He would add Betty to his Book of Grievances. Stupid woman. Why hadn't she minded her own business?

Vilya arrived the following week at seven o'clock with a bag of weights and equipment.

"Good evening, Syderney. You are ready to vork?" she asked holding out an exercise band which was wrapped round both meaty fists like a garrotte.

"A cup of tea?" he asked in desperation.

"Water vould be good please. It is important to keep hydrated."

"Yes, yes!" he said rushing into the kitchen. How long could he spin this out? He turned the tap on very slowly.

She followed him and stopped at his liquidiser.

"Vat is this?"

"I've been experimenting. It's a salad smoothie."

"I may taste it?"

"Oh yes, indeed!"

Before Vilya had arrived, he'd been considering what to eat and had decided he didn't have time for a meal. One thing led to another and he'd wondered about developing smoothies for busy people on the go. A search on the Internet told him someone had beaten him to it but he'd had another idea. Suppose he blended the starter, main course and dessert together? Many people appreciated gourmet meals but didn't have time to sit down and eat one. With his Three Course Smoothies, they could enjoy a complete meal through a straw while they were on the go. Disappointingly, his fridge had only yielded some wilted salad, a tiny piece of Brie and a large onion. He'd liquidised the lot. When he'd removed the lid of his blender, the smell had hit him like a punch on the nose. He was writing his shopping list for the next day, when the doorbell rang and Vilya had appeared with her rubber garrotte, bringing his mind firmly back to the present.

Now, she removed the top of the blender which

Sydney had rammed back on earlier. She didn't flinch. Instead, she dipped her chunky finger in the brown sludge and sucked it.

"Mmm," she said, an appreciative expression on her square face. "I may have more of it?"

He almost tripped over his feet in his rush to get a glass and disregarding the smell, he poured the entire smoothie into it.

He managed to stall for fifteen minutes, while she drank and he told her about his idea. Nevertheless, it took a week for his muscles to stop complaining and he was dreading his next session. There was no point trying to cancel; Vilya knew where he lived.

Then Sydney had an idea. He'd arrive at the gym two hours early with some tools hidden in his gym bag. Once he'd gained access to the boiler room, he'd make a few adjustments to valves, thermostats – basically, anything he could twiddle. With no water and with soaring temperatures in the gym, they'd be forced to close and he'd offer to fix the problem, but by the time he'd finished, it would be too late to train. All he'd have to worry about then, was his final session, the following week. How he'd get out of it, he had no idea. Perhaps he'd catch the plague. Or move house.

"Mr Jugg, you're early! I've been phoning you," said Betty when he entered the reception. "I'm sorry but Vilya's resigned. Would you believe it? Just like that! Apparently, she's got some hotshot new business idea and she's setting up a new company. Three Course Smoothies or somesuch. I'm sure I can find another personal trainer for you though..."

Sydney was too stunned to answer. That square-jawed, sadistic monster had stolen his idea!

"Mr Jugg?" Betty said. "Are you okay?"

He nodded.

"You can have a refund if you'd prefer. Oh, and I wonder if you'd leave your business card please? My shower's not working at home. If you have time, perhaps you'd come and look at it?"

He nodded, unsure whether his relief that Vilya had gone was greater than his fury at her stealing his idea. There would be plenty to write in his Book of Grievances tonight! He might even buy a new notebook dedicated to Vilya Chekarova.

"Mr Jugg? Your card...?"

He handed one to her silently. Yes, there would be plenty to write on the subject of the personal trainer. Perhaps he ought to have a page for Muscle Bounders Gym too. After all, they'd sent her round to his house. In fact, it was Betty's fault. *She* already had a page and he'd be sure to add this insult.

If you could come round tonight," Betty said, "I'd really appreciate it and I've made Shepherd's Pie, if you'd like to stay for dinner..."

She smiled shyly.

"D... dinner?" he spluttered.

"Well, only if you'd like…" she was now blushing.

"That would be lovely," he said. Perhaps he'd been a bit hasty putting Betty in his Book of Grievances. He'd tear her page out when he got home… later… after dinner at her house.

"Is There Anybody There?"

Betty Bentwhistle stared at the flyer someone had left in the reception of Muscle Bounders Gym.

Ichabod Bunch stared back at her from the leaflet with mesmerising eyes.

Ichabod Bunch

Clairvoyant and Medium Extraordinaire

Let Ichabod connect you with those you no longer see

Thursday 28th March at Basilwade Community Hall

Betty couldn't think of anyone she no longer saw and who she wanted to connect to. But it wouldn't matter, she could still go along for the spectacle… and those compelling eyes. She would ask Sydney if he'd like to go.

Sydney Jugg had been to Betty's for dinner on four occasions. He'd also fixed her shower and mended a dripping tap. And he'd mentioned he might look at her U-bend or P-trap or something. Exactly why he was going to inspect it, she'd no idea but it was another excuse to have him to herself for the evening. She'd spotted him weeks ago when he'd joined the gym and had been assigned Vilya Chekarova as his personal trainer. Betty had never taken to the rude woman and she felt sorry for

Sydney who was obviously not used to training in a gym. If it'd been up to her, she'd have found a much gentler personal trainer for Sydney... but it hadn't been up to her – she was simply the receptionist. And then Vilya had stolen Sydney's brilliant idea for a new business. It had failed miserably, but Betty wasn't surprised. Vilya was neither intelligent, nor a 'people-person'. If Sydney had been allowed to develop his three-course smoothie idea himself, Betty had no doubt he would be a millionaire by now.

But Sydney was brimming with ideas and given the support of a good woman, he would one day be a successful businessman. And she was just the sort of good woman to offer him the support and encouragement he needed. Indeed, she was the sort of good woman to look after him for the rest of his life – if he'd let her.

But one thing at a time. While marriage was firmly on her radar, she suspected it was not on his... yet. She wasn't sure what a 'Spring Chicken' was but it suggested something young and fresh. These days, she was feeling more like an old boiler. In a few more years, she'd have gone off the boil completely and she would be doomed to a lifetime on her own.

"A medium? What for?" Sydney asked, as he helped himself to another spoonful of Betty's beef goulash.

"Oh, you know," she said, passing him the rice, "it might be fun."

"But don't mediums talk to dead people?"

"Mmm."

"Is there a dead person you want to talk to?"

"No, not really. I just thought it might be interesting… and I've bought the tickets. I thought I'd try lamb hotpot on Thursday and then we could stroll down to the hall…"

"Lamb hotpot? That's my favourite. Oh, well okay, if you'd like to go. Wouldn't you prefer to go on your own while I have a look at your stopcock? It needs a bit of attention."

"It would be so nice to go together and I'd like you to meet some of my friends…"

"Oh, all right."

Sydney was torn. On one hand, it was lovely to be spoiled and plied with delicious meals. On the other, he had a feeling Betty was offering more than stews and pot roasts. Occasionally, she let slip a comment which implied she expected them to be together many years hence. Yes – marriage was definitely on *her* mind. During the long hours at work when he was bending and soldering copper pipe, he mulled the idea over. Would it be so dreadful? Betty wasn't bad looking. She fed him, fussed over him and generally made him feel special. So special that it had been many weeks since he'd opened his Book of Grievances and he was sure that he was beginning to forget some of the injustices which he'd experienced. But – and it was a large 'but' – he didn't want to feel he was being manoeuvred into something which hadn't been his idea.

The lamb hotpot had been followed by apple pie, and Sydney felt it would be rude not to accompany Betty to Basilwade Hall. She'd said that some of her friends would be there but when they arrived, she seemed to know everyone. They sat next to Betty's best friend, Florrie Fanshawe.

"Pleased to meet you," said Florrie, shaking Sydney's hand and fixing him with a determined stare which seemed to say *Don't even think about messing with my best friend, Betty.*

Mystical music suddenly began to play, heralding the appearance of Ichabod Bunch. He swept on to the stage, his voluminous, black cloak billowing behind him and then seizing the microphone with a bejewelled hand, he raised one arm and with fingers outstretched as if reaching for something, he closed his eyes and began to hum.

"What the…?" muttered Sydney, looking at the ridiculous, cloaked man.

"Shhh!" said several of the people round Sydney.

He glanced about. Surely people weren't taking the charlatan seriously?

But, apparently, they were.

Ichabod Bunch was suddenly silent. His eyes flew open and the audience gasped. Slowly he turned his head, allowing his gaze to sweep across the eager faces, as if searching for someone special.

"Oooh!" several women said as his staring eyes rested on them momentarily and then moved on.

Ichabod placed his hand on his chest, the stones in his rings catching the light as he breathed in and out.

"I'm receiving a message." His eyes closed and most of the audience leaned forward in anticipation.

"Yes, I am thinking of the letter M," he said in the voice of one whose mind was meandering through the clouds and stopping periodically to chat to angels.

"Ooooh!" said the audience.

"Does the letter M mean anything to anyone?"

Nearly every hand shot up.

Ichabod's eyes flew open.

"Ooooh!" said the audience.

"You," he said pointing at the woman next to Florrie Fanshawe, "what does the letter M mean to you?"

The woman patted her hat to ensure it was in place and rose. "I'm Maud Wilson and this is my daughter Mary…" she indicated a young woman sitting next to her whose face flushed crimson as everyone's eyes swivelled from her mother to her. "Maud and Mary. That's two M's," she said triumphantly.

"Excellent! Excellent!" said Ichabod. "That M was coming through very strongly and now I can see why. The message I'm receiving is from someone with thinning hair. A pleasant looking gentleman who cared for you deeply when he was amongst us."

"That must be my Harold!" Maud said excitedly, nudging Mary with her elbow.

"Yes, that's correct," said Ichabod, "he tells me that Harold is his name. He says that things may have been cloudy for some time but there are blue skies ahead." Ichabod turned away but Maud hadn't finished with him.

"So, can you tell me if my Mary is going to find a husband at long last?"

"Mum!" whispered Mary, aghast.

"Oh, and ask Harold what he did with the silver sugar tongs," added Maud.

"Mum!"

"Well, when you've got the ears of the dead, Mary, it's best to get as much out of them as you can. Harold never gave me any hope when he was alive. It took until after he'd died for him to offer me blue skies."

"Oh!" said Ichabod with a great show of disappointment. "I'm afraid Harold seems to have gone, but he sent his love."

"Typical!" said Maud with a sniff.

"Shhh!" said Mary; head bowed to hide her flaming cheeks.

Ichabod had moved on.

"I have a clear picture of a ginger cat. Does that mean anything to anyone?"

"Ooooh!" said the audience.

Nearly every hand shot up.

A week later, over steak and kidney pudding, Betty said she was thinking of booking a clairvoyant session for them both with Ichabod Bunch.

"Whatever for?" Sydney asked, his mouth full of suet pastry and meat.

Betty was vague. "Oh, you know," she said.

Sydney didn't know.

All he knew was that during the last seven days, Betty had hardly uttered a sentence which didn't contain "Ichabod said..." or "Ichabod thinks..." She was remarkably well informed about Mr Ichabod Bunch.

"More?" asked Betty, piling another spoonful of pudding on his plate. Sydney decided he'd wriggle out of the session later. But first, he'd finish his dinner.

Unusually, she'd hastily cleared the table as soon as his knife and fork touched the plate and suggested they wait a while for coffee.

"Why?" he asked.

"Oh, you know."

Again, he *didn't* know.

Almost immediately, the doorbell rang and Betty, with eyes sparkling and cheeks aflame, sprang up to open the door.

It was Ichabod Bunch.

So, the proposed session had actually been booked for this evening!

For a second, Sydney toyed with the notion of walking out. That would teach Betty to manipulate him! But there was something in the way her eyes lit up at the mention of that man's name that stirred feelings deep inside Sydney. Why didn't her eyes glow like that for him?

He would stay. After all, he'd met Betty first and he was jolly well going to stake his claim. You couldn't get steak and kidney pudding like *that* anywhere in Basilwade.

Vagueness and generalisations, thought Sydney, how could Betty be taken in by such rubbish?

Ichabod had spoken for twenty minutes but said precisely nothing and Sydney had just started to fidget, when the clairvoyant suggested he see them both privately.

Betty agreed at once.

"You can wait in the kitchen, if you like, Sydney," she said.

Reluctantly, Sydney left. He listened at the door but could only hear deep mumbling and girly, giggles. Betty didn't laugh like that at any of his jokes!

He sprang away from the door and pretended to inspect the cactus on the windowsill when Betty came to fetch him.

"Ichabod will see you now," she said, her face glowing. "Oooh, he's so—"

Sydney rushed out before she could finish the sentence and enlighten him.

"Ah, sit down, Sydney," said Ichabod. "I understand you'd like me to probe the future for you…"

"No," said Sydney, "I'm quite happy to wait until it happens."

"Excellent! In that case, my work here is done." Ichabod rose.

"What?"

"I propose to see the lovely Betty next Tuesday for another session. I trust that's all right with you?"

"What? Well, no actually. That's not all right with me."

"I see," said Ichabod sitting down. "Well, in that case, you will need a very good reason why she should miss our appointment." He nodded wisely. "It appears to have escaped your attention, but Betty is looking for someone with whom she can share her future. If, for argument's sake, she should find someone between now and Tuesday evening, there would probably be no need for her to consult me."

Ichabod rose again. "Oh, and by the way…" he paused theatrically, "grudges and grievances are not attractive. Not to women, anyway. It might be time to get rid of the book."

"B… book?" How did he know about Sydney's Book of Grievances? A lucky guess, surely?

But Ichabod had swept out of the room.

When Betty appeared with coffee, Sydney had made up his mind. She wouldn't be keeping the appointment next Tuesday with Ichabod Bunch. Sydney would propose marriage to her. Not today, of course, that would be rather premature, but he'd hint at it before Tuesday so she'd have no need to see the clairvoyant, and then when the time was right, he'd get down on one knee and pop the question.

He opened his eyes wide in an Ichabod-like expression and fixed Betty with his gaze, trying to convey the depth of feeling he was experiencing.

"Are you all right, Sydney? Your face has gone all weird. Have you got indigestion?" she asked.

Going Freelance

With the palm of her left hand placed against her cheek, Betty Bentwhistle wiggled her ring-finger, trying to draw her aunt's attention to the new engagement ring. Aunt Edie, however, was oblivious to the sparkling chip. But then her spectacles were remarkably smeary. Not surprising really, since she cleaned them with anything that came to hand.

'Ere, cut that out, Betty my girl!" Len Malone rose gingerly from his armchair on the other side of the common room and hobbled towards them. "You're dazzling me with that flashy diamond!" He grinned, displaying a brilliant white set of dentures.

"Congratulations are in order then?" he asked, taking her hand to inspect the ring.

"Congratulations? What for?" Aunt Edie asked.

"Looks like your niece has caught herself a fella," said Len. "If I'd been forty years younger, I'd have popped the question meself!"

"Engaged?" asked Aunt Edie. "Since when? And to whom?"

"Yes," said Betty proudly holding out her hand to display the ring, "since yesterday and to Sydney Jugg."

"Jugg!" said Aunt Edie with distaste. "What kind of name is *Jugg?"*

"Don't take no notice, love," said Len, "she's a bit crabby because the elections for Leisure

Organiser are coming up and she's worried she won't get in again."

"So, are you going to tell us where you met this young man?" asked Aunt Edie.

Betty told them how she'd met Sydney at Muscle Bounders Gym and how she'd been told by a clairvoyant that she would shortly be marrying the man of her dreams.

"A clairvoyant?" Aunt Edie asked. "You don't believe in all that nonsense, do you?"

"But Ichabod's readings always come true," Betty said, "and he's got lovely eyes."

"*Ichabod?* What kind of name is *Ichabod?*"

"Not Ichabod Bunch?" Myrtle Mayer, the elderly lady next to Aunt Edie said, leaning over to join the conversation. "I saw him at Basilwade Community Centre last month. Oooh, those eyes!"

"I know," said Betty, "they're mesmerising, aren't they?"

Aunt Edie glared at Myrtle. "No one asked you!" She turned back to Betty. "So far, I know more about Ichabod Bunch than I do about Sydney Mugg."

"*Jugg*, Auntie, his name is *Jugg*."

"Mugg! Jugg!" said Aunt Edie crossly, then shaking her head, she added slowly, savouring the words, "Mrs Betty Jugg… Oh dear."

"Well, I think you'll make a lovely mug, love," said Myrtle, adjusting her hearing aid.

"Nobody asked you," said Aunt Edie.

"Who cares," replied Myrtle, "everyone knows you're a crosspatch. And don't think you're going to get my vote for Leisure Organiser!"

"What? I'll have you know my Beetle Drive was the most popular event this year."

"Who told you that?"

"Vernon Pollard."

"Well, there you are then. How can you trust a man who pours custard on his salad?"

"It was a mistake! He thought it was mayonnaise."

"But he ate it."

"Well…"

Betty crept out of the Willows Retirement Home wondering if she could avoid sending Aunt Edie a wedding invitation.

Edie Bentwhistle needed to arrange a memorable event before her term as Leisure Organiser concluded, or she'd never get voted back in. But what could she do? She'd run bingo, beetle drives and whist evenings. However, they were becoming dull and predictable. She'd tried poker but Matron banned it after Vernon Pollard ran out of matchsticks and started peeling clothes off instead. And the talent show had been too stressful. Some of Len Malone's jokes had been a bit racy, and he'd ignored Matron's orders to come off stage. He later said he was pumping with adrenaline and hadn't heard her which may have been true as whatever had been coursing through his veins had been sufficient to allow him to forget his arthritic knees as he ran round the room chased by Matron. And as for the incident with Dora and Rex in the broom cupboard, the less said about that, the better.

And then Edie had it. She would get the clairvoyant and medium with the strange name that Betty and Myrtle had been raving about although she'd have to be circumspect when she told Matron who was rather prim and proper about such things.

By the time she had the opportunity to ask Matron, she'd forgotten the name of the medium.

"Icarus Punch," she said uncertainly, "he's a sort of spiritual... um person."

Matron looked doubtful. "I'm not sure I hold with anything like that."

"Actually, he's a magician," said Edie, pleased at her flash of inspiration, "you know, pulling rabbits out of hats, that sort of thing."

"Oh, I see, well, that's different. Yes, of course you can hire him. What a good idea! Is there any chance you could book him yourself, please Edith? There's going to be an inspection of the home next week and I'm rather snowed under."

"Leave it to me," said Edie.

She suspected she hadn't remembered the name correctly but dared not ask Myrtle. The fewer people who knew, the better, in case her idea was stolen by someone else. She telephoned Betty.

"Ichabod Bunch," said Betty, "why d'you want to know?"

"Oh, I just wondered."

By the time Matron discovered there were no hats or rabbits, it would be too late and it might even finish the evening with a swing if Matron chased Ichabod round the room. He would probably be faster than Len and such a finale would round things off nicely. Yes, she would surely be voted in as Leisure Organiser once more.

Betty had been correct. Ichabod's eyes were indeed mesmerising, Edie decided as she led him to the linen storage room to change. She wondered how much power they could exert over Matron, if she were to leave the reports she was completing in her office and come to find out how the 'magic show' was going. And there was always the possibility that one of her staff members would alert her to the real identity of Ichabod Bunch – but hopefully not until the evening was over.

"Well, if you'll allow me ten minutes to dress and prepare myself, dear lady…"

"Oooh, yes," said Edie, gazing at Ichabod adoringly.

"So, if you'd just go outside while I change…"

"Oooh, yes," she said and slowly backed out of the room, unwilling to break eye-contact, "I'll be right here waiting," she called through the door that Ichabod hastily closed.

Arm chairs had been cleared from one end of the sitting room and arranged in rows.

"What's the idea of this? I can't see the telly," complained Vernon.

"Shh! He's coming!" said Edie who was at the door watching for Ichabod to emerge from his changing room.

"Now!" she said, waving both hands at Len who was manning the CD player.

"It's not working," said Len frenziedly twiddling knobs and stabbing buttons.

Suddenly a few notes of music drifted out of the CD player and cut through the expectant hush.

"Oh, my favourite," said Dora, "Ol' Man River."

"Oops, sorry, that's the radio," said Len.

"Do something!" squeaked Edie.

Len rose and began to hum the *Last Post.*

Vernon staggered to his feet and standing as upright as he could, he saluted.

Rex stood up. "Just off to the gents." He winked at Dora, held his hand up with five fingers splayed, tapped his watch and jerked his head in the direction of the broom cupboard.

"He wants to meet you in the broom cupboard in five minutes," said Myrtle to a blushing Dora.

"Shut up!" said Edie, hopping from foot to foot. "He's here!"

And just as Ichabod swept through the door in his voluminous cloak, Len – still humming – found the correct button on the CD player and fell silent as esoteric music wafted round the expectant crowd.

"Oooh! Look at those eyes!" said Myrtle.

Ichabod raised one arm, his fingers outstretched as if reaching for something. Suddenly, the audience gasped when his eyes flew open and he allowed his gaze to sweep across the eager faces as if searching for someone special.

"Oooh!" said Dora.

"I'm being given a message about something blue," Ichabod intoned, "does that mean anything to anyone?"

"Len's jokes are blue," said Vernon.

"My husband once had a blue tie," said Myrtle. "He hated it. It was a Christmas present."

"I've got a blue rinse," said Dora, fluffing up her hair coquettishly.

"Does the letter B or P or D mean anything to you?" he asked Dora. "I have a gentleman wishing to make contact."

"Oh, yes, it could be Brian, Peter or David. Or Bernard, Percy or Des. Or—"

"Quite," said Ichabod. "I believe it's Brian. He wants to say hello—"

"Well, that's rich, coming from him! He couldn't wait to say goodbye!"

"Ah, erm, perhaps it was Peter. Yes, it's *Peter* who wants to send you his greetings."

"Well, you can tell him from me he can keep his

greetings! I've never been so embarrassed in all my life! And you can tell him from me…" she tapped her chest and pursed her lips belligerently, "that silk underwear looked ridiculous! Oooh!" she said to Ichabod. "You said you could see blue, didn't you? That underwear was blue… or was it pink? Well, he looked ridiculous in it anyway!"

"Sadly, Peter has gone," said Ichabod, "but I'm getting a message about a special day at the seaside. Does that mean anything to anyone?"

Every hand shot up.

"Well, the evening could've gone worse," remarked Myrtle tipping Cornflakes into a bowl, the following morning.

"I'm not sure it could've," snapped Edie.

"How were you to know Matron would come by so early in the evening to see the show," Vernon asked, "or that she used to teach Ichabod when he was a school lad?"

"Small world, eh?" said Len. "That weren't very professional of her to call 'im a fraudster, were it? I thought he were brilliant. I don't know how he does it. How could he have known what I did with that ice cream in Bognor in 1954? I never told anyone. It were quite spooky."

"I know," said Myrtle "it was a bit harsh of Matron to say 'once a fraudster always a fraudster' though, weren't it?"

"He had such lovely eyes," said Dora, "eyes to die for."

"Rex nearly died for 'em," said Len. "He nearly suffocated in that broom cupboard waiting for you while you were playing fast and loose with Ichabod and his eyes."

"Rubbish!" said Dora. "There's plenty of air in that cupboard. He just fell asleep. He wasn't struggling for breath, he was snoring."

"Who'd have thought Matron used to be a teacher? On second thoughts, she is a bit school-marmy, isn't she?" said Myrtle. "And it's no wonder Ichabod changed his name. *Norman Wormwood* isn't quite as exotic, is it?"

"I thought Matron were going to grab him by the ear and drag him off to detention," said Len, "but he escaped faster than I did at that talent show."

Edie cleaned a blob of butter off her spectacles with a jammy napkin. "There's no way I'm going to be re-elected Leisure Organiser now," she wailed.

"Don't worry about it," said Dora.

"Easy for you to say. It gave me something to get up for in the morning."

"There's always a solution," said Myrtle pulling a flyer out of her pocket. "Why not go freelance?"

On Saturday evening Matron telephoned the duty nurse to find out how the Scrabble evening she'd organised was progressing. She didn't have enough time to arrange social activities but at least if she did it herself there would be no more fiascos like the previous week.

"What do you mean the sitting room is empty?" She asked horrified.

"There's a flyer on one of the chairs, I'm not sure if it might be a clue. It says *Ichabod Bunch, appearing at Basilwade Community Centre on Saturday Evening...*"

So App-ealing

"Rex Parker, you're moving that glass with your finger!" said Edie Bentwhistle, jabbing him with her elbow. The tumbler on the Ouija board jerked to a standstill as he lost contact with it.

"You horrible little man," said Myrtle, "it's not moving at all now you've taken your finger off it! I might have known the spirits wouldn't be sending us messages about doughnuts. Why don't you go and jostle a few brooms with Dora? The pair of you seem to be spending more and more time in that broom cupboard together."

"That's not true," said Dora.

"Well, the cleaner's gone off work with stress after finding you two in there. Poor girl! She's only eighteen and she was quite traumatised.

"Honestly," said Rex, "the youth of today. They've got no backbone, no stamina."

"Whereas backbone and stamina seem to be something you have plenty of…" said Myrtle.

"Well, if you want to know the truth," said Dora, "he's not as—"

Before she could enlighten everyone, the door opened to reveal Matron. She snapped the light on. "What's going on here?"

"Just a friendly game of, umm… Scrabble?"

"In the dark?" asked Matron.

"It's not completely dark. It's only darkish."

"It's dark," said Matron in her *don't contradict me* tone of voice.

"We're saving electricity, Matron."

"I'm not a fool, Len Malone! I know an Ouija board when I see one. I thought I'd made myself very clear the other day after the disgraceful incident with that clairvoyant. The Willows Retirement Home does not permit activities connected to the occult."

"It's just a bit of fun, Matron," said Len.

"Not as far as I'm concerned, Len Malone! Now, I insist you abide by my rules or go elsewhere."

"It's like being at school," whispered Len.

"It's worse," replied Dora.

"I suggest you all find a new pastime because I am confiscating this." Matron scooped up the Ouija board, tucked it under her arm and strode out of the room.

"We've still got the glass," said Myrtle.

"What good's that? The only spirit that glass has been acquainted with is the miniature bottle of Pernod Rex smuggled in and drank neat before Matron discovered it."

"Not an experience I shall be repeating," said Rex. "It stripped off the inside of my mouth and stomach and I think it dissolved one of my teeth."

"Find a hobby, indeed!" said Dora. "Every time we discover something interesting, Matron puts the blocks on it!"

"Not every time," said Len.

"What d'you mean?"

"She only stops the things she knows about but she don't know everything," Len said with a smirk.

"What d'you know that Matron doesn't?"

"I've got a new hobby."

Eventually, after much tapping of the side of his nose, Len couldn't resist telling.

"I'm learning to sail."

"Well unless it's a model boat in the bath, I don't see how. You haven't been further than Basilwade town centre since Christmas," said Edie.

"My nephew's got a boat moored down at Slee-on-Sea and he's lent me some books. He said as soon as I'm good enough, he'll let me take it out."

"You can't learn to sail from books! You need to practise on the water."

"Well, that's where you're wrong," said Len. "These days you can learn anything using technology. I've got an app on my phone."

"App? What's an app?" asked Myrtle.

"It's what he takes every afternoon, after lunch," said Dora.

"Very funny," said Len. "Anyway, I don't nap after lunch. I have dry eyes and my blinks are just longer than other people's."

"So, what is an app then, Len?" asked Myrtle.

"He doesn't know," said Edie, "he's just showing off."

"I do! I've got an app called 'Hello Sailor' and it's taught me all sorts of things."

"I'm sure it has although I bet it hasn't taught you how to sail," said Dora.

"I'll prove it has," said Len. "Let's go sailing on Monday."

"You let them go *where*?" Matron asked her senior nurse, Hettie.

"Slee-on-Sea. You were busy with the inspectors but Len and Dora assured me you wouldn't mind." Hettie backed away. She recognised Matron's scowl and the steely tone.

"Of course, they said I wouldn't mind! That's their modus operandi."

"Their mo… what?"

"Oh, never mind!" snapped Matron.

"Well, I'm sure they'll be all right."

"All right? Of course, they won't be all right!"

"But Slee-on-Sea is a really sleepy little place – a few quaint fisherman's cottages, a pub, a church, a fish and chip shop and that's about it."

"A church?" asked Matron. "Did you say church?" her eyes were now narrow slits.

"Yes. A lovely little Norman church if I remember correctly. They can't get into trouble in church, surely?"

"Does it have a graveyard?"

"Yes, why?"

Matron jerked her desk drawer open and fished about for her car keys.

"You're in charge while I'm out, Hettie, and for heaven's sake, don't let anyone else leave the home before I get back."

"But Matron, where are you going?"

"Down to the graveyard before they dig someone up or summon all the spirits from Valhalla."

"Matron, they're just a group of elderly people! Are you sure you're not getting things a bit out of proportion?"

"So, I was getting things out of proportion, was I, Hettie?" Matron asked later that evening.

"Well, they weren't exactly robbing graves."

"It would only have been a matter of time," muttered Matron.

"But they weren't anywhere near the church."

"I know," said Matron, "I worked that out for myself when the sister at Basilwade Hospital informed me the coastguards had taken them to A&E."

"I hope you're satisfied, Len! You nearly drowned us!"

"Oh, don't exaggerate, Dora! You're such a drama queen!" said Len.

"Drama queen? How dare you?"

"Yes, steady on, old chap!" said Rex. "You only have to look at the list of injuries we've sustained to see what an ordeal we've been through. The coastguard said he'd seen people knocked overboard by a swinging boom but never every single person on board."

"Well, I told you to space yourselves out and not all sit on the same side of the boat. But did you listen? No! It was mutiny from the instant we set sail."

"Set sail?" said Dora with a sniff. "We went aground immediately. Still, the coastguard said it was just as well we hit that sandbank because with high tide in the evening and the strong currents, we'd probably have drifted out into the North Sea."

"Well, I think you're all very ungrateful," said Len. "When was the last time you had so much excitement?"

There was silence for a few moments.

Rex winked at Dora. "Last Monday, in the broom cu—"

"I really can't remember," said Dora tossing her head and avoiding eye contact with Rex. "Oh and by the way, you owe me fifty quid, Len."

"What for?"

"I bought a new pair of deck shoes and they're covered in mud"

"I'm sure we can clean them up," said Len. "We'll let them dry and then brush them. They were brown anyway."

"They were beige, not brown and we can't clean them up. They're still in that sandbank. I stepped right out of them."

"Before anyone puts in a claim for new clothes," said Len, "remember I could charge each of you for chartering my ship."

More silence.

"So," said Myrtle, "how much will it cost you for boat repairs to your ship?"

"Ah, well, under the circumstances, my nephew has been very understanding. He says the insurance company will pay to put the damage right but he's banned me from sailing it ever again."

"Thank goodness for that!" said Edie. "Well, I hope that's taught you a lesson, Len."

"It's certainly taught me not to waste my expertise on ungrateful people like you lot!"

"No, I meant I hope it's taught you to forget the idea you can learn something complicated like sailing from an app on your phone."

"The trouble with you old folk is you've been left behind in the Technological Revolution. You're all dinosaurs! But some of us have vision. Some of us are tech savvy!"

"So, you're going to carry on sailing with your app, are you?"

"No, as it happens," said Len. "I'm not sure sailing's really my thing. I realised that when I went under for the third time. It suddenly came to me. I've got a new hobby. And I've got a new app."

"Tiddly-winks?" asked Edie.

"I think it's the Cr-app," said Rex.

"Oh, very funny!" said Len.

"Actually, Rex, that was quite funny," said Dora.

Rex beamed and shuffled closer to her.

"It's app-solutely fapp-ulous!" said Rex.

"What an app-alling joke!" said Dora.

"But you have to app-reciate it!" said Rex.

"Oh, ignore them," said Myrtle. "What is your new app?"

"It's called 'Going Deeper'," said Len.

"What's it for?"

"It's going to train me to be a deep-sea diver…"

No Saints at All Saints'

Hettie Forbes-Snell decided against catching the evening bus from outside the Willows Retirement Home where she was senior nurse. After such a difficult day, she wanted time to unwind before she reached the vicarage. She was smarting at the way Matron had treated her. While the Inspectors had been probing the kitchen, the bedrooms, the accounts and the medical cupboard, Matron had accompanied them, leaving Hettie in charge. It hadn't been Hettie's fault that a group of the more trying guests had ended up in Basilwade A&E after a boating accident earlier that day but Matron, who'd been as jumpy as drops of water in a sizzling frying pan, had been unnecessarily critical. And Hettie had been very hurt.

After all, today had been painful enough without a tongue-lashing from Matron.

Today was her birthday.

No one had remembered, not even her brother, Wilbur, but that wasn't surprising because he was always so preoccupied, and if she was honest, totally self-centred. He might be the parish vicar but he was certainly no saint. Mrs McSquirtle didn't help either. She was the housekeeper although her title was a misnomer because she did very little in the way of keeping house. She couldn't *keep* much of anything – the vicarage accounts, secrets, her temper and often her balance. This was mainly due to her partiality to a nip of medicinal brandy every now and again, and often in between as well. She spoiled Wilbur by baking numerous batches of shortbread but often forgetting to do the laundry, clean the house, do the shopping, tidy the garden or prepare meals.

"Please have more charity, Hettie, dear," Wilbur would say when she complained. "Mrs McSquirtle has a heart of gold."

"And a liver full of your brandy," Hettie would mutter.

"What's that, dear? Speak up!"

But Hettie would simply get on with whatever needed to be done, thinking dark thoughts about the small, barrel-shaped woman she privately thought of as *Big Mac*.

When Hettie finally opened the front door, the smell of burned food assaulted her nostrils, darkening her mood. In an ideal world, it was at this point that family and friends would suddenly leap out of cupboards shouting "Surprise!" and there would be an enormous cake and balloons saying *Happy 50th*. However, she didn't have any family other than Wilbur, and not many friends. And, this was not an ideal world, this was All Saints' Vicarage, Basilwade.

"Is that you, Hettie?" Wilbur called from the study. Without waiting for an answer, he added, "Bring me a slice of toast with my cuppa, will you?

I'm meeting the ladies of the Mothers' Union in a few minutes. I'll eat dinner when I get back."

A dinner, she knew, he expected her to prepare, to replace whatever Big Mac had incinerated.

By the time Wilbur returned, Hettie had made Shepherd's Pie, cleaned up most of the charred remains of whatever it was that Big Mac had put in the oven hours before, and was about to run a bath for herself.

"Hettie, would you be a dear and help with the travel arrangements for the Mothers' Union annual outing to Bognor? You know how good you are at that sort of thing… Hettie? Hettie?"

She crept upstairs pretending not to have heard and locked herself in the bathroom. She wanted to cry. The only celebration of her fiftieth birthday would be a lonely bubble bath.

"Hettie are you still in there?" Wilbur called ten minutes later as he rapped on the bathroom door. "I desperately need your help to look up some coach prices on the Internet. You know how useless I am on that computer."

Hettie took a deep breath and sank beneath the mound of bubbles.

The water had gone cold and her skin was wrinkly before she got out of the bath but by now Wilbur would be asleep. She dried herself and crept along the corridor towards her bedroom accompanied by Mrs McSquirtle's snores and Wilbur's squeaks and grunts. She would be up and out of the vicarage before either of them woke in the morning but they would both be home all day, so perhaps between them they would organise the MU trip. However, she knew they wouldn't. Wilbur would spend all day organising his stamp collection and thinking about Sunday's sermon while Big Mac would bake shortbread. The arrangements would still be there to do when she got home.

Hettie climbed into bed. She was too tired and too dispirited to read her book that evening. Usually, it was her only escape from normal life. Tonight, she didn't want to be reminded that there was such a thing as *escape* because it was a luxury she knew wasn't available to her. It was so unfair. She was locked into her life with no prospect of getting away. Hettie looked at the clock. It was two minutes past midnight. Her birthday was over. She lay awake until the early hours, thinking. Something had to change and the time was now before it was too late.

The following evening, Hettie left work promptly. Most of the guests had been rather subdued after their brief stay in hospital, and that morning, Matron had made her a cup of tea which was probably the closest she'd come to giving Hettie an apology, so it hadn't been a bad day.

"Is that you, Hettie? Wilbur called from his study.

Hettie sniffed the air. No smell of burning. In fact, no smell at all which meant that either Big Mac had made salad for dinner or more likely, she hadn't got around to preparing anything.

"Hettie! Is that you?"

"Yes, Wilbur."

"Thank goodness! I've got a meeting with the choirmaster and I need to know you've progressed with the MU outing. Oh, and I wonder if you could bring me a cup of tea before you start dinner..."

By the time Wilbur returned from his meeting, Hettie had made toad-in-the-hole and worked out prices for the trip to Bognor. The sooner it was done, the sooner she could run a bath, climb into bed and escape into her book.

"So, the coach will arrive at the carpark nearest the seafront at about eleven o'clock and then you can go to a café for tea or walk along the promenade. I've booked you in for lunch at—"

"Hettie! You keep saying *you. I* shan't be going. I'll be much too busy."

"Well, I've booked *them* in for lunch then," said Hettie.

"No, no! I can't send the ladies on their own! I was hoping you'd volunteer to accompany them. You know what a mess we got in last time when we lost three ladies."

"Since we're being particular about pronouns, *we* didn't lose three ladies, *you* lost three ladies. *I* was working that day. *You* were in charge."

"Oh, don't be so petty, Hettie! Anyway, I've arranged the trip for a Saturday so you won't be working."

"No, *you* didn't arrange the trip. *I* did."

"Sometimes you're impossible! I expect you'll be reminding me of how I borrowed your fluffy penguin when I was seven, next…"

"*Took*," muttered Hettie. "You *took* my fluffy penguin."

"What you need is a lot more charity and forgiveness, Hettie!"

She sighed. She might as well give in because she knew he wouldn't let up until she'd agreed to go on the trip.

"All right," she said, "I'll go with them."

"That's the ticket! I'm sure you'll have a lovely time. The ladies of the MU are wonderful. Well, all except for Florrie Fanshawe. She's a bit of a madam. But the others are fine. Oh, and Mrs Myers. She can be a tartar too…"

Hettie didn't reply. She'd gone into the kitchen to start dinner.

"Well, if they don't call you Saint Hettie," said the driver, as he pulled into the seafront carpark in Bognor, "they definitely should. I've never met anyone with such patience."

"There's no point getting cross with the ladies," said Hettie, "but I'm definitely no saint."

"So, what's your secret?"

"Secret?" Hettie asked, her cheeks aflame. "I don't have a secret," she said quickly, hugging her bulging rucksack to her chest.

"I just meant you kept your cool despite that woman with the hair that looks like shredded wheat telling everyone what to do in the case of earthquake or tsunami."

"Ah, that's Mrs Myers, the church warden. She's always prepared for every eventuality. And that means everyone else has to be prepared too, whether they like it or not."

"She weren't prepared when that woman threw up over her though were she?"

"True. Although she did manage to catch most of it in her hat."

"Yeah, I'll give her full marks for that," said the driver, nodding his approval.

The day had been exhausting. Hettie had to remove three ladies from the amusement arcade where they'd got into an argument with the manager.

"This place is a modern-day Sodom and Gomorrah!" said Mrs Myers as Hettie apologised to the man and led the ladies away.

"Yeah, sod 'em," said Florrie.

"And Gomorrah," said Mrs Yates.

Hettie took them to the Cheeky Cockle Café where the others were waiting to start lunch. A headcount revealed that someone was missing and Hettie's sharp ears heard a loud sobbing emanating from the Ladies, which proved to be the missing person. Nervous Miss Stibbins was inconsolable after a freak gust of wind had blown a dish of jellied eels down her front and candyfloss into her hair earlier that morning. She wept as Hettie tried to pick the sticky, pink bits from her hair and mop her front with a serviette but finally, she allowed herself to be led, red-eyed to the place Mrs Myers had saved for her. On reflection, it would have been better if Hettie had swapped places with Miss Stibbins and saved her the lecture from Mrs Myers about hurricanes and evacuation procedures. It was fortunate that one of the ladies carried smelling salts in her handbag and was able to revive Miss Stibbins.

After lunch, Hettie let the ladies loose on Bognor once more for an afternoon stroll but despite dire warnings of being left behind if they weren't back at the coach at five o'clock, three women were late. Hettie finally found Mrs Myers, Florrie Fanshawe and Mrs Yates, in the amusement arcade haranguing the manager again.

"Out," Hettie shouted, her arm extended and her finger pointing at the door, "or we'll leave you behind!"

The open-mouthed ladies followed her.

"I shall tell her brother how she's treated us," whispered Mrs Myers. "It's outrageous!"

The other two nodded.

But Hettie didn't care. She'd brought thirty-four women to Bognor and she would send thirty-four back to Wilbur – come what may. No one would be lost on her watch. And if they weren't happy with the way she'd treated them, they could take it up with her brother when they arrived in Basilwade.

She wouldn't, however, be accompanying them home. After shepherding them on to the coach, she thanked the driver.

"I'm so sorry to do this to you, but I won't be travelling home with you. I hope the ladies behave."

As the driver spluttered with indignation, Hettie climbed out of the coach and walked briskly away, clutching her rucksack tightly. Inside, she had her toiletry bag, a few clothes, her passport, a fluffy penguin and a train ticket from Bognor to London St. Pancras. From there, she would travel by Eurostar to Paris.

And then? Well, she'd make up her mind when she got there.

A Meal of Biblical Proportions

Sundays are busy days for vicars. And the Sunday following the Mothers' Union outing to Bognor was particularly demanding. After morning service, everyone who'd been on the trip wanted to give Reverend Wilbur Forbes-Snell their personal report on the day. Everyone, except Wilbur's sister, Hettie, who'd been remarkably quiet on the subject. It wasn't until tea time that Wilbur noticed he hadn't seen Hettie all day. And the more he thought about it, the more he realised he hadn't seen her since she'd left with the MU ladies the previous morning.

With any luck, she was in the kitchen making sandwiches for tea although Mrs McSquirtle had obviously been baking as he could smell shortbread cooking and his mouth watered. He'd go and see if tea was ready. And he must remember to remind Hettie to put out some pickled onions – something that however many times he reminded her, she always seemed to forget. There wasn't a meal he could think of that wasn't improved by the addition of a pickled onion – or two.

Mrs McSquirtle was sitting at the kitchen table, her head resting on her arms and a glass of brandy by her elbow.

"Mrs McSquirtle! I've asked you not to start on the brandy until five o'clock. It's not seemly." He tapped his watch, "It's only four o'clock."

"Whssshht!" she said, her voice slurred. "I didn't open thish until after five o'clock yesterday." She indicated the empty brandy bottle, "and remember, it'sh for medicinal purposes."

Wilbur sniffed.

"I believe your shortbread is beginning to burn, Mrs McSquirtle. Where's Hettie?"

"Hettie who?"

"My sister, Hettie!"

"How should I know?"

"Really, Mrs McSquirtle! Such rudeness! I'm going to have to rethink the brandy arrangements if I don't have some cooperation from you."

Mrs McSquirtle sat up, snatched the bottle and held it to her chest, then blinked rapidly as she tried to focus on the vicar. "You have my full corrororpation… corropercation… coorrorpation—"

"Where's Hettie?" Wilbur cut in.

"Dunno."

"When did you last see her?"

Mrs McSquirtle's left eye looked up at the fluorescent fitting on the ceiling. Her right eye swivelled in its socket and then gazed longingly at the cupboard beneath the sink where she'd hidden several bottles of brandy.

"Um…"

"Did you see her this morning before service?" Wilbur asked.

"Oh yesh," she said with as much certainty as she

could muster. She couldn't remember anything that had happened earlier that day but it was fairly safe to assume that Hettie had been at morning service. Where else would she be?

"Was she at lunch?"

Mrs McSquirtle couldn't remember having had lunch.

"Ummm…"

"Come, come, Mrs McSquirtle, you must remember if Hettie was here at lunch time."

The housekeeper's eyes narrowed. "Beggin' yer pardon, Reverend, but don't you remember seeing her at lunch?"

"I would have remembered if I'd been home but as I told you this morning, I was invited to lunch with Mrs Myers. Now, did you or didn't you see Hettie?"

"No," said Mrs McSquirtle. She was on safe ground now. The vicar hadn't been here, so he couldn't say what she might or might not have seen.

"I suggest you get the shortbread out of the oven before it burns," Wilbur said as he swept out of the kitchen.

"Yesh," she said, laying her head back on her arms.

On Monday, Wilbur called the police, and Constable John arrived several hours later. A brief search of Hettie's bedroom revealed a letter on her bedside table which clearly showed that she had left of her own free will.

Dear Wilbur,
I'm leaving.
Regards,
Hettie

There was some doubt about the date of her departure because the coach driver said that Hettie had not boarded the coach back to Basilwade on Saturday afternoon and several of the MU ladies had corroborated that. So far, the only person to claim to have seen Hettie on Sunday, had been Mrs McSquirtle but the constable was disinclined to believe her since during her interview, she claimed to have seen bright lights in the garden and small people wearing silver space suits who had led Hettie away. The housekeeper had then fallen asleep and he'd been unable to rouse her sufficiently to check any more facts.

"In conclusion, Reverend," said Constable John, tucking his notebook back in his pocket, "Miss Forbes-Snell appears to have left of her own free will, so I'm afraid this isn't a matter for the police."

By the following Saturday, Wilbur was in a very dark mood. So was Mrs McSquirtle who was about to hand in her notice when she realised her brandy supply would almost certainly dry up – and another employer, assuming she could find one – would probably not be as lenient as the vicar. No, she was duty-bound to stay and look after him. Even if he had turned into a bad-tempered and unreasonable man. She silently cursed Hettie. There had been no word from her other than one postcard from Paris saying she was fine. *Well, good for Hettie,* Mrs McSquirtle thought crossly because *she* certainly wasn't fine. The Reverend had become more demanding since his sister had gone, expecting breakfast, lunch, tea and dinner at regular intervals and to make matters worse, he'd found her hidden supply of brandy and was rationing her. She'd explained that the brandy was medicinal but it had fallen on deaf ears. Wilbur had offered to pray for her medical condition but had not been any more generous with his brandy allowance. And to make matters worse, the Bishop and two churchwardens were coming for dinner on Saturday. A dinner she was expected to cook.

And Wilbur was unusually agitated. Actually, *snappy*, might be a better description.

"Dinner," he said, "has to be perfect. Nothing less will do."

She'd pointed out that the stress was upsetting her medical condition and that a large brandy would ensure the success of the dinner on Saturday. Wilbur had been rather harsh, quoting chunks of the Bible which featured fire and brimstone. And now Mrs McSquirtle was angry – *stressed* and angry. And an angry, stressed Mrs McSquirtle was not a rational being. Her integrity and her fitness as a housekeeper had been called into question.

It was too much.

It was war.

And Mrs McSquirtle had no intention of losing.

On Saturday evening, Wilbur hovered by the front door ready to receive the Bishop and churchwardens while Mrs McSquirtle finished the preparations for the dinner she had dubbed her 'Religious Experience'.

Wilbur had been too flustered to question the housekeeper more closely and moaned yet again that Hettie was being selfish and ought to come home.

In the kitchen, Mrs McSquirtle placed two pickled onions in each bowl and covered them with tinned tomato soup. Reverend always said that there wasn't a meal that couldn't be improved by adding pickled onions, *so let's see how he likes this*, she thought.

"Samson Soup," she announced proudly, as she placed bowls in front of Wilbur, the Bishop, Mrs Myers and Mr Chubb.

"Samson Soup?" asked the Bishop.

"It's very biblical," said Mrs McSquirtle. "My inspiration is from the Book of Judges,"

"Ah, Samson – the man who was tricked into cutting his hair by Delilah."

Mrs McSquirtle nodded.

"Well, I hope the soup doesn't have hair in it," the Bishop said and laughed heartily at his own joke.

"Oh, ho, ho! Very good my lord," said Mrs Myers.

The Bishop beamed at Wilbur. Wilbur looked uncertainly at the housekeeper.

"I've done my best to re-create the part where the Philistines gouged out Samson's eyeballs," Mrs McSquirtle said.

Mrs Myers had been scrutinising the pickled onion she'd fished out of the soup when she heard the word "eyeballs". She screamed and dropped the spoon and onion back into the soup bowl with a splash. The Bishop, who'd already swallowed some of the soup, gagged, and Mr Chubb who was well-known for laughing at inappropriate times, giggled hysterically. Wilbur looked as though he'd sat down on a pole. His eyes bulged and he emitted a high-pitched squeak.

"Not to everyone's taste, then," Mrs McSquirtle said, gathering up the bowls and placing them on her tray. "Never mind. I'll bring in the next course."

"Wh… what is the next course?" asked the Bishop gripping his serviette nervously.

"Salome's Surprise," said Mrs McSquirtle over her shoulder as she left the dining room. She reappeared several minutes later with a large silver platter, on which was a domed cover.

The Bishop gasped. "When you said *Salome,* did

you mean the Salome who demanded the head of John the Baptist on a platter?"

"The very same," said Mrs McSquirtle with a satisfied smile. She reached for the handle on top of the cover to raise it.

"Stop!" screeched Wilbur. He leaped up, grabbed her by the shoulders and propelled her into the kitchen. By the time he got back to the dining room, the Bishop, Mrs Myers and Mr Chubb had gone, although he could hear the sound of giggling wafting on the breeze. Wilbur was at a loss. If only Hettie were here to deal with this. What should he do? Well, obviously the dratted housekeeper must be fired and he certainly wouldn't give her a reference. Yes, he would do it tomorrow.

Mrs McSquirtle put the Egyptian Trifle back in the fridge. It was her tribute to the Ten Plagues of Egypt. She'd always said the good thing about trifle is that you could make it out of pretty much anything and to this one, she'd added a few pickled onions just for fun. The other thing she knew about trifle is that it doesn't matter how carefully it's served, everything gets mixed up and it always looks a mess. She'd planned to have fun pointing out pieces of kiwi which could easily be mistaken for frogs – and currants which could pass for flies or lice depending on size. Oh well, she thought, Wilbur can have the trifle tomorrow. She would still be employed tomorrow. She knew that. Despite the fact that he was – even now – planning to fire her.

But he wouldn't.

She had taken the precaution of hiding his supply of pickled onions in the cellar along with his stamp collection and the girlie magazines that he'd hidden in his wardrobe. She'd left one of the magazines, on his bed. When he returned it to its hiding place, he would discover the others were missing and would know that she knew about them. The cellar was the one place that Wilbur feared to tread since he had a phobia about spiders – especially the extremely long-legged, fat-bodied ones which thrived in the vicarage cellar. Now that Hettie had gone, who would dare to brave those terrible arachnids? Only trusty, dependable Mrs McSquirtle. If he sacked her, he'd have to persuade one of his parishioners to go into the cellar to retrieve his pickled onions and stamps which were on the bench right next to his girlie magazines.

Mrs McSquirtle climbed the stairs to bed. The washing up could wait until tomorrow when Wilbur could do it. She had won the war and things were going to be very different around here from now on. Pouring herself a double brandy, she placed it on the bedside table and climbed into bed. Just for devilment, she'd put a dead long-legged, fat-bodied spider in Wilbur's bed and he should discover it in about… she checked her watch… five minutes time when he went to bed. The scream would probably break every window in the neighbourhood and send the dogs in a five-mile radius into a frenzy. Smiling, she rammed her ear plugs home, finished the brandy and pulled the bedclothes over her head.

It is Better to Give than to Receive

"Why are there so many apologies tonight?" Reverend Wilbur Forbes-Snell asked the three members of the Parochial Church Council who'd arrived at the vicarage for the meeting.

Mrs Myers, the churchwarden, who was also secretary, looked at the list of people who would not be joining them. "I believe there's a gripping episode of *East Enders* on tonight," she said.

"Saints preserve us!" said Wilbur. "Such lack of dedication! I shall have words next Sunday."

"It's lucky some of us have dedication to spare," said Mrs Bakewell with a smug smile, "and some of us have such wonderful news, nothing could've kept us away, eh, Reverend?"

"Look at her batting her eyelashes at the vicar," whispered Mrs Myers to the other church warden, Mr Chubb.

"Indeed! It's disgraceful. She's so *obvious!* No wonder they call her Bakewell Tart," he said, leaning towards Mrs Myers and speaking out of the corner of his mouth.

"Look at her pouting. Honestly!" whispered Mrs Myers.

"She looks like a trout," replied Mr Chubb speaking from behind his hand.

"Right," said Wilbur, "let's begin."

"Sorry I'm late," said Mr Sykes, the organist, who

rushed into the room holding a handkerchief to his nose and sat down next to Mrs Bakewell, "I've got a terrible cold."

She pulled her chair away and glared at him. "Kindly keep your germs to yourself."

"Right," said Wilbur, "I think we can accept the minutes of the last meeting, so perhaps we can turn to item one on our agenda."

"Oh, yes, let's," said Mrs Bakewell, rubbing her hands together.

Wilbur beamed. "One of Mrs Bakewell's Premium Bonds has won a large prize and she's very generously offered to donate a sum of five thousand pounds to All Saints' Church."

The two churchwardens and organist gasped. Mrs Bakewell blushed and looked down modestly while Wilbur beamed at everyone.

"And now, we have the happy task of deciding what the money should be spent on," said Wilbur. "My suggestion would be silver candlesticks for the altar—"

"Oh," said Mrs Bakewell with a frown, "I was thinking more of a stained-glass window."

"You can't put new windows in willy-nilly," said Mr Sykes, "All Saints' is an ancient building."

"I wasn't suggesting we do anything *willy-nilly*," said Mrs Bakewell with a sniff. "There's a plain glass window in the porch which could do with some colour."

"But the window doesn't need replacing," said Mr Sykes. "I vote we use the money to carry out some urgently-needed repairs to the organ."

"But no one will be able to see what the money – *my* money – has been spent on," said Mrs Bakewell.

"Let's have something everyone can enjoy," said Mrs Myers.

"Stained-glass can be enjoyed by everyone," said Mrs Bakewell.

"Everyone adores the organ," said Mr Sykes.

"I don't," said Mr Chubb, "I find it depressing. And I don't think the choir like it either because they always sing faster than the organ so they can get the whole thing over with."

"Nonsense," said Wilbur, holding his hands up for silence, "now, let's not fall out over this wonderfully generous donation. If I could direct your thoughts back to silver candlesticks… I'm sure everyone would enjoy those."

"I wouldn't," said Mrs Myers. "There's enough silver in the church and it's hard to clean. It takes me hours to polish what we've got."

"Quite right," said Mr Sykes, "we've got enough silver."

"How would you know? I don't ever see you cleaning the church," said Mrs Myers.

"Dust upsets the delicate skin on my hands. I have to keep them healthy to play the organ."

"It might be nice to have a week without any

organ music," said Mr Chubb wistfully.

"You are a Philistine, Mr Chubb. I receive nothing but praise for my playing and that's why I vote we spend the money on the organ."

"There's nothing wrong with the organ," said Mrs Myers. "I think it's the organist that needs replacing."

"Ladies and gentlemen, please!" said Wilbur raising his hands for silence. "Well, we've heard what Mrs Bakewell and Mr Sykes want. What do the churchwardens think we should spend the money on?"

Mrs Myers paused from taking the minutes. "I'd suggest we replace the notice board and repaint the church hall."

"I repainted the church hall last year," said Mr Sykes, glaring at her, "and I'll have you know, my hands blew up like balloons after being in contact with that paint!"

"Well, you should have concentrated more on putting it on the wood than your hands. You made a very dismal job of it, if I may say so."

"No, you may not say so. I didn't see you climbing ladders to do any painting."

"You know I suffer from verdigris," Mrs Myers said crossly.

"I think you'll find it's vertigo you suffer from," said Mrs Bakewell, sniggering. "Verdigris is that green stuff that covers copper, isn't it, reverend?"

"Supercilious cow!" whispered Mrs Myers to Mr Chubb who pressed his knuckles to his mouth to stifle a giggle. He was renowned for his inappropriately-timed, high-pitched laughter which had earned him a ban from public services such as baptisms, weddings and funerals.

"Well, thank you, Mrs Myers for your suggestion. Now, the only person whose idea we haven't heard, is Mr Chubb… Mr Chubb?"

But Mr Chubb was giggling uncontrollably and if he had an idea, he was unable to say.

"If the glass broke in the porch window, we wouldn't need permission to replace it, would we?" said Mrs Bakewell.

"It isn't broken," said Mrs Myers "and unless you take a sledgehammer to it, it isn't likely to be."

"I was speaking theoretically. If it accidentally broke, we could replace it, and a stained-glass window would look wonderful. I've drawn a design. Look reverend, what d'you think?" Mrs Bakewell slid a sheet of paper towards Wilbur.

"What's it got on it," asked Mrs Myers, "her coat of arms?"

"Is it a big pie?" asked Mr Chubb trying to conceal his laughter by blowing his nose.

"A tart, you mean," said Mrs Myers.

"How dare you call me that!" said Mrs Bakewell.

"Ladies, ladies! Please!" said Wilbur. "I'm sure Mrs Myers wasn't calling you a tart, Mrs Bakewell."

"Takes one to know one," said Mrs Myers looking down her nose.

"If we can't come to a consensus, I think I'm going to have to put my foot down and insist on candlesticks," said Wilbur.

"And as the benefactor, I'm going to insist on a stained-glass window. I've set my heart on it," said Mrs Bakewell.

"This is ridiculous," said Mr Sykes. "I vote we put it to the vote."

"How can we vote? We need to narrow the choice down a bit."

"Well," said Mr Sykes, "I vote we—"

"Please!" said Mrs Bakewell. "Will somebody shut *Votey McVote Face* up! I'm sick of his voice! *I'm* donating the money, so *I* should have the final word!"

"Mrs Bakewell! Really! There's no need for name-calling, I'm sure we can settle this amicably," said Wilbur sliding her cheque under his book in case she tried to snatch it.

"*Votey McVote Face?"* shrieked Mr Sykes. "Well, that's rich, coming from *Bloaty McBloat Face!"*

"Mrs Bakewell, Mr Sykes, I'm shocked!" said Wilbur, his hands held up in front of him in an attempt to calm things.

"It looks like Reverend is surrendering," whispered Mrs Myers to Mr Chubb who exploded into guffaws and left the room with tears rolling down his cheeks.

"How dare you!" said Mrs Bakewell grabbing Mr Sykes' tie and thrusting the knot upwards until his eyes bulged. "Now shut up!" she said as she sat down. Mr Sykes scrabbled at the knot trying to lower it.

"Mrs Bakewell... please!" squeaked Wilbur. He was close to tears.

"I do apologise, Reverend," Mrs Bakewell said in silky tones, as she smoothed her hair back in place.

The obstruction to Mr Sykes virus-infested airway set a large sneeze in motion. It was later argued that he hadn't found his handkerchief in time although Mrs Bakewell claimed he'd done it on purpose when the forceful expulsion of virus-laden air from Mr Sykes nostrils hit the side of Mrs Bakewell's face.

Mrs McSquirtle, Wilbur's housekeeper, poured tea into Wilbur's favourite cup, placed some shortbread on the saucer and slid it across the table towards him.

"I'm sure they'll all be chums again tomorrow," she said.

Wilbur cradled his head in his hands. "I don't think so, Mrs McSquirtle. In fact, I wouldn't be surprised if Mrs Bakewell doesn't press charges for assault after Mrs Myers shoved her. You should've seen them pulling each other's hair. They were like animals – all fur and claws. And then Mr Sykes stepped in to separate them but one of them bit him on the hand. You should have heard the fuss! He called 999 for an ambulance. Goodness knows what he said to the emergency services but when the paramedics arrived, they appeared to believe his hand had been bitten off by a rabid animal. At least the appearance of uniformed men calmed down Mrs Bakewell and Mrs Myers. But Mr Sykes was furious the paramedics treated the ladies' cuts and scratches more seriously than his bite."

"I'm sure it'll all come out in the wash," said Mrs McSquirtle. "Pickled onion?" she asked, passing him the jar.

He munched silently on an onion for a few minutes, then added, "I'm afraid too many harsh words were spoken last night. And Mr Sykes is threatening to sue. I tried to insist the two ladies shook hands before they went home but honestly, Mrs McSquirtle, the language! And they've all resigned from the PCC."

"Oh dear. Well, never mind. I expect they'll be here tomorrow asking to be reinstated."

"No, I don't think so. If you'd seen their faces when they left you wouldn't think that, and you know what it says in Psalms 109 verse five…"

"Umm, remind me?"

"And they have rewarded me evil for good, and hatred for my love."

"Well, never mind. I always say it's darkest just

before dawn. Here, Reverend, have another pickled onion. It'll all be better in the morning."

She poured a measure of medicinal brandy in his tea and topped up her own.

Superhero Worship

Persephone Perkins fluffed up her blonde hair, smoothed the dress over her hourglass figure and knocked at Mr Chubb's front door, taking care not to chip her blood-red nail varnish. Her real name was Phyllis but having come to Basilwade with her son – leaving Mr Perkins in another part of the country – she wanted to reinvent herself. And the name *Persephone*, she decided, rather suited her.

She'd moved into the house next door two weeks before and during that time hadn't met her neighbour, although a letter addressed to *Mr C. Chubb (Churchwarden All Saints)*, had mistakenly been delivered to her house, informing her of his name. From the uproarious laughter that frequently emanated from next-door, she guessed he was large and jolly, with chubby, red cheeks, so she was surprised when a small, skinny man with round, horn-rimmed glasses opened the door.

She held out her hand. "Persephone Perkins," she said, "from next door. Pleased to meet you at last."

"Charlie Chubb. Likewise," he said, straightening his glasses and blinking at the goddess before him.

She gave him her most dazzling smile. "I'm sorry to bother you, Charlie, but I wonder if you could do me the teensiest favour..." She held two red nails together to indicate how small the teensiest favour would be. "I've got an important meeting and my babysitter's let me down… So, I wondered if you'd look after my son for a while. I'd be soooo grateful." She pouted and fluttered her eyelashes.

Charlie's cheeks reddened. He wasn't used to women and especially not glamourous females like the one who now stepped forward and removed a speck of dust from his cricket jumper. When Charlie was nervous, he laughed which made him more nervous, until he became hysterical. As he choked back the giggles which were threatening to erupt, Persephone took advantage of the silence.

"What a kind man you are to help me out like this!"

"B… but… I don't know the first thing about babies… And I'm on my way to a cricket game," said Charlie, shock managing to stifle the laughter.

"You dear man!" said Persephone, patting his chest as if he'd told a humorous joke. "He's six-years old and he loves cricket, don't you?" she said reaching behind herself to drag out a small boy dressed in a yellow and black striped tee-shirt and jeans.

Persephone patted the small boy on the head. "This is my son, Ulysses. You won't be any trouble, will you, U?"

The young boy scowled. "I might," he said.

Charlie shook his head; eyes wide in panic. "I'm going to play cricket, I won't be able to look after—"

"Oh, he loves cricket! Don't you, U?"

"No," said the boy.

"And he doesn't need looking after, he'll play with his doll—"

"Action figure!" said Ulysses, glowering.

"Action figure," said Persephone, leaning forward to straighten Charlie's glasses. "You might need to clean these if you're going to play cricket," she said, "the lenses are steaming up."

Charlie giggled and turned puce.

Persephone spun on her spiky stiletto heel and after stooping to kiss Ulysses, she minced down the path.

"Behave for Charlie, won't you, U?"

Ulysses wiped the crimson lipstick smear off his cheek and looked up expectantly at Charlie.

"My name's Waspman," he lisped through the gap where his two front teeth should have been.

"Quite," said Charlie. "Well… err… laddie… if you'd like to come in, I'll get my things."

"Ah, Mrs Myers!" Charlie said as he entered the cricket pavilion bar. "I wonder if you could do me a favour, please." He indicated Ulysses. "This is U… err… my next-door neighbour—"

"Waspman!" said Ulysses.

"Quite," said Charlie with a giggle. "Yes, well, I'm supposed to be looking after him but obviously I can't while I'm playing. You don't think you could mind him for me, do you?"

"I don't need looking after!" said Ulysses. "I'm a Superhero."

Mrs Myers looked doubtful. "I'm not sure how I'm going to keep a child amused, Mr Chubb."

"Oh, he's got a doll… err… an action thing to play with. He'll be no trouble."

Mrs Myers scrutinised the action figure. "What on earth is that?" she asked, curling her lip in distaste. "It appears to be dripping something disgusting."

"It's Wormwoman," said Ulysses. "She's a superhero an' she can escape from anywhere by exuding slime."

"Well, she'd better stop exuding it all over my floor!" said Mrs Myers.

Charlie took the opportunity to back out of the bar and made for the changing room where Mrs Myers couldn't follow.

"Brenda!" yelled Mrs Myers.

Brenda Baskin came rushing from the kitchen, wiping soapy hands on her apron. She was almost as tall as she was round with a smile which lit up her face.

"Ah, Brenda!" said Mrs Myers. "You're used to children, aren't you? There's a little chap here who we need to look after for Mr Chubb." She hurried into the kitchen leaving Brenda to deal with the boy.

"What've you done with him?" Mrs Myers asked when Brenda came into the kitchen.

"Poor lamb," said Brenda, "apparently his mother's dumped him on Charlie so she can have a facial."

"Yes, yes! But what's he doing now? He's not still dripping slime over the floor, is he?"

"Don't you worry, Mrs Myers, he's playing nicely with that doll. I've told him I'll take him a biscuit when I've found the pickled onions. Vicar'll create like anything if there aren't any of those strong ones he likes for tea."

Brenda placed a bowl of super-strength pickled onions on the table in the gap between the vol-au-vents and sausage rolls. She could have sworn the cucumber sandwiches had been there next to the cheese and pineapple on sticks. Perhaps Mrs Myers had moved them. She had a few biscuits for the boy – but he was nowhere to be seen. Rushing to the door, she asked the spectators who were outside watching the match if the boy had left the bar, but if he had, no one had noticed. As she turned around, she saw the flicker of a shadow beneath the enormous table on which the tea was being set. She gently raised the tablecloth.

"What're you doing under there? And why've you dismantled Mrs Myers' cucumber sandwiches?" she asked, pointing at the empty plate, the heap of thinly sliced cucumber next to his knee and the buttered bread triangles which were scattered on the floor.

"Cucumber's disgusting," he said flicking the pile with his finger.

"Well," said Brenda gathering everything up and piling it on the plate, "lots of people *do* like cucumber sandwiches, so I'll thank you to leave them alone. Here, these are for you." She handed him the biscuits. "Keep your hands off the food and don't touch the pickled onions or you'll have Reverend Forbes-Snell to answer to."

Ulysses took the biscuits.

"What d'you say?" asked Brenda. She had seven grandchildren and six great-grandchildren, so she knew about teaching children manners.

"When can I go home?" said Ulysses, spitting biscuit crumbs through the gap in his teeth.

"Why are you washing those cucumber slices?" Mrs Myers asked.

"Health and Safety. You can't be too careful these days," Brenda muttered, placing her considerable girth between Mrs Myer's inquisitive eyes and the plate of opened and empty sandwiches. If she was careful, she'd be able to clean the fluff and grit off the cucumber and reassemble the sandwiches before Mrs Myers realised what had happened. Brenda remembered the slime on the boy's hands and wondered whether the buttered triangles would stand a quick dip in the washing up bowl but decided they'd probably disintegrate. She'd just have to check each piece as she reassembled the sandwiches and scrape off any slime if necessary. The last sandwich had just been placed on the plate, when she heard choking coming from the bar.

"I told you to keep your hands off those pickled onions!" Brenda said when she took in the scene of the upturned pickled onion bowl and the stricken, heaving boy with his mouth open and hands wrapped round his throat.

"Oh, lordy!" she said, rushing towards him. Wrapping her arms round the boy from behind, she pulled him into her cushion-like body, performing the Heimlich Manoeuvre. Ulysses gagged, forcibly ejecting the onion from his throat. It bounced twice and rolled under the table.

"Well, I shan't be washing that one!" she said, scooping up the other onions and dropping them in the bowl. "Now, sit down and wait for me to clean these up."

To her relief, when she returned, Ulysses was sitting where she'd left him, although he was subdued after his recent encounter with the pickled onion. She wasn't sure if the tears in his eyes were as a result of choking, the indignity of being seized in the Heimlich Manoeuvre or because of vicar's extra-strength onions.

"Why don't you go outside and watch the cricket?" she asked in her best grandmotherly tone.

"'S boring. I hate cricket!" His sulky expression returned.

"I see. Well, why don't you tell me all about… that?" she asked, pointing at Wormwoman, trying to disguise her distaste at the Barbie-like doll dressed in a brown, shiny outfit which was smeared with goo.

For the first time since he'd arrived, Ulysses became animated and told her about Superhero Wormwoman and her exploits.

"I see," said Brenda, feigning interest. "So that goo helps her escape from her enemies."

"Yeah! It comes out here," he said pointing to a small hole in her back "and I can fill the slime extruder here," he said opening a small flap beneath the hole. "But Mum wouldn't let me bring my spare slime." He frowned. "Wormwoman's got other tricks too!" he added.

"Are they as messy?" Brenda asked, frowning at the slime on the floor.

Ulysses ignored her question. "An' I've got Spiderman, Waspman, Bugboy an' Grubgirl at home! But Mum wouldn't let me bring them."

"That's an awful lot of creepy-crawly Superheroes," she said.

"Brenda! Where are you?" called Mrs Myers from the kitchen although from her tone, she might just as well have said "Brenda! Come here!"

"Why don't you take Wormwoman outside for

some fresh air while I help Mrs Myers?" she asked the boy.

He looked doubtful but before he could speak, there was a deafening crash.

"Oooh!" gasped the spectators outside and someone shouted. "Six! Good old Chubby!"

Brenda hurried to the door and poked her head outside. "Well, Charlie's on form! That's another six he's scored and it's the third window he's broken in the pavilion this season. He'll be Man of the Match… again and I expect we'll slaughter Wickleston… again."

"What?" Ulysses asked, his voice rising in incredulity. "That weedy man from next-door broke a window?"

Brenda nodded.

"He hit the ball all that way?" He pointed at the far-off figure of Charlie standing by the wicket, giggling uncontrollably.

"Charlie's a demon batsman. Mind you, he's a demon bowler too. You wouldn't think it to look at him, would you?"

"He doesn't look like he's good at anything," Ulysses said. "I thought he was a wimp."

"Well, I always find appearances can be deceptive," she said tartly.

"Is he some kind of Superhero?" Ulysses asked in awe.

"Absolutely," said Brenda, "in fact…" she paused

and looking right and left as if checking for eavesdroppers, she whispered, "don't tell anyone but he's actually Cricketman."

"Cricketman!" said Ulysses, his eyes wide and his mouth open. "Can I go and watch him play?"

"Absolutely," said Brenda with relief as Mrs Myers bellowed from the kitchen.

"Brenda! Why are vicar's pickled onions in the washing up bowl?"

Persephone balanced her mobile phone against her ear with her shoulder and splaying her fingers in front of her, she studied her nails.

"Hello," came the disembodied voice from the phone's speaker. "Phyllis?"

"Hi, Mum. I'm Persephone now, by the way, not Phyllis. Please try to remember."

"Well, how are you and little Ulysses? You haven't answered my last few calls? Are you settling in okay?"

"I'm fine, thanks, Mum. I've just been so busy." She pulled a tendril of hair and allowed it to spring back into place.

"And how's Ulysses?"

"He's fine."

"Can I speak to him?"

"He's at the cricket club with his new friend, I'm afraid."

"Oh, lovely, he's found a friend!"

"Yes." Persephone stroked an eyebrow back into position. "Charlie Chubb from next-door. U thinks he's wonderful."

"That's good. Do they go to the same school?"

"School? Oh, no! Charlie's an adult. Between you and me, I think there's a bit of hero-worship going on which is rather odd because Charlie's such a puny little man. Definitely not hero-material but apparently, he's a brilliant cricketer. But the good news is, U doesn't play with those Superhero dolls as often – not now he's taken up cricket."

"How marvellous! He's never shown any interest in sport before."

"I know! I'm not sure he's any good at it but he wanted me to buy him cricket gear and he wears it all the time which is a bit of a pain as it needs a lot of washing to keep it white. I drew the line at buying him horn-rimmed glasses like Charlie though."

"Ulysses doesn't need glasses, does he?"

"Oh no, he just seems to like copying Charlie. I don't mind the cricket but I wish he wouldn't imitate Charlie's laugh. It's driving me crazy…"

Playground Justice

The small boy with the dark curls sat at one end of the playground bench; shoulders hunched and head down. Around him in the autumn sunshine and strong breeze, children ran, skipped and spun in a flurry of playtime activity like the coloured, papery leaves which were falling from the trees.

"The little darlings'll be as 'igh as kites by the time the bell goes," said Lizzie Turnpike.

She and Brenda Baskin were playground supervisors at All Saints' Junior School and both ladies had noticed that strong winds at playtime resulted in very excitable children going into the next lesson. The pupils would barely calm down by lunchtime, only to find themselves out in the windy playground again.

"*He* won't be high as a kite," Brenda said, nodding her head at the lone boy on the bench, "poor lad."

"He's the new kid, isn't he?" asked Lizzie. "The one with the weird name. Something like Urology or Uber, or something."

"Ulysses," said Brenda. "Ulysses Perkins."

"Oh yeah. Honestly, the names some parents make up! Ulysses, indeed! Whoever's heard the like?" asked Lizzie, her eyes roving expertly over the children, searching out mischief. "Look at *that*..." she strode across the playground pointing her finger at a large, sandy-haired boy who'd seized the ponytail of a much smaller girl and was attempting to swing her around.

"Tommy Watkins!" Lizzie bellowed. "That is dangerous behaviour. Let go at once!"

Tommy stopped dragging the small girl although he didn't relinquish his grip on her hair.

"I'm jus' playin', Miss. It ain't dangerous!"

"Don't argue with me, Tommy Watkins. When I say it's dangerous, it's dangerous! Now let go of Tara's hair."

Reluctantly, he released the ponytail.

Tara's hands flew to her head as if to make sure her hair was still there. On finding her ponytail in place, she balled her fists and swung at Tommy.

"See!" said Lizzie handing the snivelling Tommy a tissue and leading him back into school to staunch the nose bleed. "I told you it was dangerous."

Brenda sat down on the bench next to Ulysses.

"Hello, Waspman," she said, remembering what he'd called himself when he'd met her at the cricket club.

The boy looked up and his smile tugged at her heart strings.

"Not playing with anyone?" she asked.

"Nah."

"Shall I see if you can join in someone's game?"

"Nah."

"It'll be the end of playtime in about two minutes and then it'll be painting. That'll be fun, won't it?"

"Nah."

Brenda sat silently for a few moments, wondering how best to get the others in his class to accept him. They were a nice group of children but Ulysses was rapidly getting the reputation of being a loner – and as Ashak, one of more popular boys, had said earlier when she'd suggested he talk to Ulysses. "He's a weirdo, Miss. Do I have to?"

"He's not a weirdo!" she'd said.

"Well his mum is," the boy said and scampered off.

Brenda hadn't known what to say.

Ashak had a point.

During Ulysses' first week at school, a succession of his mother's friends had arrived at the playground each evening to collect him. Brenda had seen Charlie Chubb there on various occasions and had imagined the wheedling that had taken place with Mrs Perkins batting those very thick – and very false – eyelashes to persuade him she had a very important 'meeting' which clashed with the end of school. It'd taken Charlie a few weeks to realise that the 'meetings' Mrs Perkins 'simply had to attend' were appointments with her beauty therapist, hairdresser or masseur – even clueless Charlie couldn't fail to notice the new nail colour, hairstyle or heady fragrance which hadn't surrounded her when she'd knocked at his door hours before, begging him to pick up Ulysses.

Brenda had been appalled at the woman's cheek in manipulating Charlie and at her apparent lack of interest in her own son. In her opinion, a parent should be there to pick up their child until he or she settled into their new school.

But she soon changed her mind the first time Mrs Perkins arrived in person. Unfortunately for the boy, it was before he'd made any friends. And after Mrs Perkins made a spectacle of herself, Ulysses was still thought of as the new boy but now he was also an object of ridicule.

Brenda had been in the playground the afternoon that Mrs Perkins had arrived in skin-tight leggings and sporty top with a rolled mat under her arm and she'd approached the various groups of mums, dads and carers in turn.

"Hello, I'm Persephone Perkins," she'd said, extending her hand to whoever would take it. "My boy's just started here. Now, I wonder if any of you would be interested in joining a yoga class? A friend of mine's just started one and she's a marvel. I've got some business cards if anyone's interested." She'd then handed them out regardless of interest.

The bell rang and the sound of scraping chairs and the occasional shout of a teacher drifted from the open windows of the school building. Shortly after, children spilled out of the doors and wove their way across the playground to whoever was waiting for them.

Persephone stood on tiptoe, craning her neck

looking for Ulysses and after a moment, her two-tone red and pink nails began to tap irritably on the rolled-up yoga mat.

"How long does this take?" she asked a tall, skinny woman who'd just arrived.

"How long does what take?"

"How long does it take until all the children are out?"

"How long's a bit of string?"

"But I need to get to yoga. Oh, by the way, if you're interested in joining a new class, here're the details," she said handing the woman a card. "It's going to be popular, so make sure you join before the class fills up. Although looking at most of these women, they've let themselves go and I don't think anything's going to get them back on track. You look like you might be quite bendy, though," Persephone said looking her up and down.

"Rosie! Over here!" someone shouted to the tall, skinny woman and beckoned her to a group of mothers, all of whom had their backs to Persephone but were peering over their shoulders with much whispering and laughter.

Oblivious to their derision, Persephone stood on tiptoe again, swaying precariously, trying to spot Ulysses amongst the hordes of children. Finally, she spied him moving almost reluctantly amongst his darting, scurrying schoolmates like a cyclist pedalling slowly down a motorway full of speeding cars. She stood higher on her tiptoes and waved her arm in a wide arc, trying to attract his attention. At last, he saw her, his eyes darting right and left as if searching for an escape route.

"U!" Persephone bellowed.

The playground froze as each person assumed that an accusatory "You!" had been yelled out which usually signalled some bad behaviour. People turned with a puzzled *Who me?* expression on their faces and several children stopped poking, pushing or jabbing those nearest them and shoved their hands in their pockets.

"U!" called Persephone again, unaware of the exhibition she was making of herself. "Come on!"

With his head down to hide his crimson cheeks from the sniggering children and open-mouthed adults, Ulysses hastened to meet his mother before she roared again.

"Yes, Brenda, I agree," said Mrs Gibbons. "Poor Ulysses isn't settling into my class at all well. Have you any suggestions?"

"I've only met him once but he got quite enthusiastic when he was talking about his favourite superheroes. Apparently, he's obsessed with them."

"Well, I could ask him to tell us about them during Show and Tell. D'you think he would? I'm sure the other children would find it interesting."

"Yes, that's an excellent idea."

Fifteen minutes before the end of school, Mrs Gibbons announced Show and Tell.

"Well, children, I'd like you to give Lucy Pelham a warm welcome as she brings her nature collection to Show and Tell."

The pupils applauded and Lucy carried a small box to the front of the class.

"And what do we have in the box, Lucy?" Mrs Gibbons asked.

"Well, Miss," said Lucy, taking the top off, "I've got some spinny things and a spider."

Mrs Gibbons took a step backwards. "Perhaps it's best not to let the spider out, Lucy."

"Oh, he's dead, Miss."

"Ah, I see. Well, perhaps you could put everything there." She pointed to the far side of her desk. "You can tell us where you found everything. Do you know what sort of spider it is? Or was?"

"No, not really, Miss. It's hard to tell." Lucy tipped the contents of the box on to the desk.

"Well, Lucy, I can see the sycamore seeds," said Mrs Gibbons from the far side of the desk. "Oh, and by the way, children, those winged seeds are known as *samaras*. Perhaps you could drop one, Lucy, to show us how they fly like helicopters."

Lucy obliged and told the class she'd found them in the local woods.

"And where is the spider, Lucy?' Mrs Gibbons asked as casually as she could. She wasn't convinced it was dead.

Lucy pushed the pile of sycamore samaras about with her finger, spacing them out.

"Umm… ah! Here's a leg, Miss," she said holding up a hair-like item in triumph. "Oh, and here's another."

"Ah, well, I think we'd better pack up now, Lucy. The bell will be ringing any minute."

"I've found another leg, Miss, shall I stay after school and glue the spider back together?"

"Well, as interesting as that would be, Lucy, I think your mummy might not want to be kept waiting."

"I don't think Lucy's mum'll shout, like the new boy's did the other day, Miss," said Tommy Watkins, setting the children giggling.

"Enough! Do I need to remind you that in this class, we are kind and we are friendly? What are we, children?"

"Kind and friendly, Miss," the class chorused.

"And sometimes weird," someone from the back whispered setting the class giggling again.

"Now, put up your hand if you would like to bring something in for Show and Tell tomorrow?" asked Mrs Gibbons.

"Oooh, oooh!" children said, trying to attract her attention with their arms extended upwards.

Ulysses hands remained in his lap.

"I think I'm going to ask Ulysses Perkins to bring something in for us."

The small boy with dark curls looked up in alarm.

"I've heard you have an interest in superheroes

and I'm sure there's a lot you can tell us about them. And I understand you have some err… action figures," Mrs Gibbons said, remembering Brenda's warning not to call them *dolls*.

For the first time, Ulysses eyes lit up with enthusiasm. "How many can I bring in, Miss?"

"Oh… um… just bring in your favourite… so long as it isn't the slimy one," she added remembering Brenda's description of the Wormwoman doll with the slime reservoir.

"How did Show and Tell go yesterday?" Brenda asked Mrs Gibbons the following morning when she saw her in the staff room.

"Not quite as successful as I'd hoped," said Mrs Gibbons.

"Oh no! What happened? Oh, he didn't bring in that slimy doll, did he?"

"No, he brought in Cricketman, who turned out to be his next-door neighbour, Charlie Chubb. Poor Mr Chubb was under the impression he'd come to watch Ulysses in some sort of show. Apparently, he thought Mrs Perkins couldn't make it and didn't want Ulysses to feel let down by not having anyone to support him. What he didn't realise was, that *he* was the object of Show and Tell."

"Oh dear. Poor Charlie, he hates being stared at. Sometimes, he gets so embarrassed, he err—"

"Laughs?"

"Yes," said Brenda, "and sometimes, it's rather... err,"

"Manic?"

"Yes," said Brenda. "Oh dear. How did the class take it?"

"Well, let's say there was much hilarity and all of it aimed at Ulysses and Cricketman. The only person not laughing was the poor lad."

Brenda looked for Ulysses at morning playtime but he wasn't on his usual bench. She'd seen him at registration, so he was definitely in school and she began to worry. Perhaps he was hiding somewhere. Walking briskly round the playground, she spotted Tommy Watkins who'd crept up on Tara Day and now had her ponytail in his chubby, grubby fingers. Since Tommy was behind her, Tara couldn't reach him, despite her flailing fists. Brenda stomped across the playground towards them but before she'd got far, she saw Ulysses step out from the bushes where he'd been hiding and tap Tommy on the shoulder. Presumably fearing adult intervention, the bully looked round only to see a small, curly-haired boy behind him. Brenda saw Tommy's lip curl in contempt as he turned back – to meet Tara's balled and flying fist. Ulysses' timid tap on the shoulder had been sufficient to distract Tommy whose grip on the ponytail had loosened. It had given Tara, who spent all her spare time at the gymnastics club, the opportunity to nimbly twist her body, putting her within punching distance of her tormentor's nose.

"Playground Justice," Brenda whispered to herself as she led a snivelling Tommy with his nose buried in a tissue to the school office to have his nose bleed dealt with.

She turned back to see what had happed to Ulysses and smiled. Tara Day had slipped her arm through his and was propelling him towards a large group of her friends. Admittedly, the same group of friends, who'd deserted Tara when Tommy had arrived but nevertheless, Brenda thought with satisfaction, their lack of support had given Ulysses a chance to shine and be the superhero of his dreams.

Politically Correct at Christmas

"A new approach to the Christmas Nativity play? Err, what exactly do you mean?" Laetitia Gibbons, class teacher at All Saints' Junior School, asked the new headteacher.

"We need to be sensitive to the needs of the entire community, Laetitia," Emma Skate replied, nodding sanctimoniously.

It was the Nativity Play planning meeting which in previous years, had lasted about fifteen minutes, allowing those present to adjourn to the *Petulant Partridge Tavern* for the rest of the night. But this evening, the five attendees had already been captive for an hour.

Ruth Abraham, who'd joined the teaching staff years before at the same time as Laetitia, sighed. The planning was not going well. She and Laetitia held similar views and had seen countless Nativity Plays performed throughout the years, and they'd both survived two changes in leadership. The latest headteacher, Miss Emma Skate, was much too young and inexperienced in Ruth's opinion. She'd only been with them one term and that had been a turbulent few weeks, to say the least. Miss Skate, or Miss Take, as Ruth had heard some of the children mistakenly call her, had tried to bulldoze her way through what had once been the smooth-running routine of the school. Alice Skipper, the head's personal assistant, had been off sick with stress twice since September and Ruth expected her to hand in her notice at any time.

The fifth person at the table was Oliver Primm, a newly-qualified teacher who was eager to make a good impression and having nothing with which to compare the current state of affairs in the school, he usually sided with the ever-confident Emma.

Alice, with pen poised over her notebook coughed nervously. Her eyes were open so wide, Ruth was afraid they might pop out.

"Are you suggesting that what we've always done hasn't been sensitive to the needs of everyone?" Laetitia asked. Her tone was icy.

"Certainly not," said Emma unaware or indifferent to the frostiness, "but this time, under my leadership, I wish the performance to be especially mindful of every single person in the community."

"I see," said Laetitia. "Well, what exactly d'you have in mind? This is a Nativity Play, so we're restricted to the main characters and setting. Of course, we could change the types of animals in the stable…"

"There will be no animals," said Emma. "The school does not tolerate animal exploitation."

"*Animal exploitation?* They're pupils dressed up!" said Ruth. "If we don't have lots of animals, many of the children won't have parts in the play."

"This year, we will *not* have animals." Emma crossed her arms.

"But what about the donkey that carried Mary?" asked Ruth.

"Donkeys shouldn't be beasts of burden," said Emma, "so definitely no donkeys."

Alice wrote *No donkeys, no animals,* on her notepad.

"Right," said Laetitia. "Well, perhaps if we decide who'll play Mary and Joseph—"

"Oh no," said Emma, "we can't be seen to favour certain children."

"We can't have a Nativity Play without Mary and Joseph," said Ruth, aghast.

"I beg to differ," said Emma, "and anyway, what about those families with only one parent or indeed, two carers of the same gender? What sort of message would we send if our representation of a family was made by a man and a woman?"

Alice wrote in her notepad *No Mary or Joseph.*

There was a pause while the three teachers tried to imagine the scene with no Mary, Joseph or animals.

"So...ooo," said Laetitia finally, "in the stable, we have a baby in a manger but no parents?"

"No," said Emma, "we can't possibly condone such health and safety violations. A baby in a manger, indeed! Definitely not. And no stable, either. The school must not give the impression that keeping babies in mangers or stables is acceptable behaviour."

Alice wrote on her list No stable, no manger, no Jesus.

There was another pause punctuated by Alice's nervous cough.

"Well," said Ruth, "the only other people in the story, are the Angel Gabriel, the shepherds and the Three Wise Men. Do we have any objections to them?"

Emma considered. "Angels?… No. I don't think we should fill the children's heads with such things. Shepherds are fine although we'll have to include shepherdesses too."

"Yes, yes," said Ruth hastily, imagining a stage full of boys in dressing gowns with tea towels on their heads and Little Bo Peeps.

"But of course," Emma added, "we wouldn't be doing our job if we didn't raise the children's aspirations. So, as well as shepherds and shepherdesses, we must have children representing other careers. Perhaps some firefighters, surgeons, lawyers, plumbers, and… well, I'm sure you get the picture."

Alice wrote in her notes *Consult careers book*.

"But, as for the Three Wise Men," said Emma, "I'm afraid not. It would send the signal that only men are wise."

"C… could we, perhaps, have Three Wise Women?" suggested Oliver.

"That would imply that only women are wise," said Emma.

"Could we have two of each gender?" asked Oliver.

"Hmm, that might work," said Emma, "although I don't like the idea of only those four people being described as *wise*. It infers the rest of the cast aren't."

"How about Two Women and Two Men of Average but Completely Sufficient Intelligence?" asked Oliver.

"Yes, Oliver, I like your thinking," said Emma.

He beamed.

Alice made a note. Her usually neat handwriting had become an untidy, jerky scrawl and her cheek began to twitch.

"So," said Laetitia, "we have *Two Women and Two Men of Average but Completely Sufficient Intelligence* as well as children dressed up to represent a variety of careers and occupations… on a bare stage."

"Yes," said Emma.

"And what should they do?" asked Laetitia.

"Oh, you know! The usual things. I thought you and Ruth had put on hundreds of Christmas shows."

"Hardly hundreds!" said Ruth crossly. "They only occur once a year."

"Well, surely you've done enough of them to know what to do without me spoon-feeding you? Now, we've spent enough time on this. I'm off to the gym, so I'll leave it in your capable hands," said Emma, slipping her laptop in her bag, putting on her coat and marching out of the staff room.

"I… I… d… don't think I can stand much more," said Alice in a quavering voice.

"I've never been so worried," Alice whispered to Ruth as she peeped through a gap in the curtains on the stage, watching excited parents enter the hall and rush forward to grab the front seats. It appeared that even the thick fog outside had not deterred them from coming.

"Shhh! The children will pick up on your nervousness and there'll be more trips to the toilets. Those elephant costumes are awfully hard to get on and off," said Ruth.

"We're all going to get fired!" Alice wailed.

"Who cares?" said Laetitia.

"I don't," said Ruth. "I'm past caring. It'd be a blessed relief not to work here anymore under that mad woman."

"You know what? "Alice sighed. "You're both quite right. Bring it on!"

"Atta girl!" said Laetitia.

But despite their brave words, Ruth noticed that Alice's facial twitch had intensified and Laetitia's eyes darted about nervously – with even more agitation than would normally be expected at a school Nativity Play.

"Right, let's line them up," said Laetitia, nibbling her bottom lip nervously.

Mary and Joseph at the head of the queue were accompanied by a child in a grey shark onesie. He had large, cardboard ears pinned to his hood, a tail attached to his bottom, and a saddle made out of sugar paper which covered his dorsal fin. With luck, the audience would realise he was really a donkey.

This is what happens when you rely on parents to provide

costumes, Ruth thought. She gave the shark-donkey a reassuring pat on the head.

The inn-keeper and her husband came next, followed by assorted animals. The elephants led the way, a lion next, then bears. The parents had been asked to provide suitable animal costumes but some had obviously not read the letter carefully, and others had only seen the word 'costume'. Two witches, one Disney princess, a Christmas elf and Darth Vader accompanied the penguins at the back of the animal procession. Several parents had angel outfits belonging to older siblings and they'd insisted their children should use the costumes, so the Angel Gabriel and six white-robed, tinsel-haloed apprentice angels followed the Dark Lord of the Sith. The final characters to go on stage were the three Wise Men and shepherds – many of whom were played by girls.

Let it not be said that All Saints' doesn't observe reasonable political correctness, thought Ruth.

She checked her watch.

It was seven o'clock.

Laetitia, with hands poised over the keys of the piano, waited for the cue. Ruth took a deep breath and nodded theatrically in her direction.

Laetitia's hands plunged.

At assembly, the following morning, Emma said, "I'm so sorry, children, I'm afraid I was caught in the fog and missed last night's Christmas Nativity performance." She gazed at Oliver, who was studying his feet; the tips of his ears had turned bright pink, "but I've heard from several parents and governors this morning that it was a great success. So, congratulations!" She beamed at the children.

"Thank you, Miss Skate," chorused the children and under her breath, Ruth muttered, "Thank you, Mistake!"

Laetitia and Ruth met in the Ladies at playtime.

"Has Emma said anything to you?" Laetitia asked as soon as she was sure they were alone.

"Nothing at all. How about you?"

Laetitia shook her head. "I think we got away with it. She obviously knows what happened last night."

"Alice told me the Chair of Governors phoned to congratulate her. Emma could hardly say she'd expressly forbidden such a performance."

"Our plan wouldn't have worked if Oliver hadn't played his part. I must admit, I wondered if he'd have the nerve to go through with it. He's so afraid of upsetting Emma. But he obviously followed our instructions to the letter. Although I must say he drives a pretty hard bargain. I've got to do all his playground duties from now until July. But at least the Nativity Play is over until next year. And from the way Emma was looking at Oliver this morning, she obviously had no idea he staged the breakdown of his car and left them stranded in the middle of nowhere until the play was over."

"Hmm," said Ruth, "if I was you, I'd tell Oliver to do his own playground duty. If Alice's information is correct, he's already benefitted from the subterfuge."

"Benefitted? What d'you mean?"

"Well, after he picked Emma up from home, he pretended to break down as we'd arranged. However, she didn't like waiting in the car in all that fog, so she insisted they went to the Wickleston Arms Hotel to wait for the breakdown van which Oliver said he'd called. Coincidentally, it's where Alice's sister works and she phoned up this morning to tell Alice all about it. Apparently, after several rounds of drinks while they waited for the breakdown van, they finally booked a room for the night."

"No!"

"Yes! And let's say that last night, the head and a junior member of the teaching staff didn't pay too much attention to political correctness."

The Life Coach

It soon became apparent why the number of pupils attending the after-school Science Club had increased dramatically that week.

"When're we going to have the taste test, Mr Primm?" one of the new children asked.

Word had got out that the usual attendees had been growing something which they were going to eat this week.

"D'you think it's going to be bacon?" someone asked.

"Or pizza?"

Several children packed up and left when Mr Primm brought out the tiny cress plants.

To those who were now gathered around his desk and who had planted the seeds the previous week, he explained about the miracle of germination and how plants feed themselves using sunlight.

"My grandad takes tablets for that," Polly said.

"Is he infected with cress?" Zoe asked.

"Nah, stupid. He takes them to bring his chlorophyll levels down, if he didn't, he might have a heart attack," Polly said condescendingly.

"What d'you do if cress has a heart attack, Mr Primm?" Zoe asked.

"That's not possible, Zoe, cress doesn't have a heart. Are you thinking of cholesterol, Polly? Plants contain chlorophyll. Humans contain cholesterol and it's high levels of cholesterol in humans which can cause heart disease."

"Possibly," said Polly, who'd lost interest and was eyeing up the gold stars Oliver kept in his desk drawer.

"Well, I think we'll finish there, children. I expect your mothers are waiting for you in the playground."

No one mentioned that they were supposed to be taste-testing the experiment.

"They're very *green*, aren't they?" a boy muttered with a frown.

Polly took one long regretful look at the gold stars and left.

Oliver glanced at the chart on the wall showing who'd earned the most stars. Polly had six so far this term. If she suddenly acquired more, he'd know where they came from.

The headteacher's PA, Alice Skipper, poked her head around the door. "Your cab's here, Ollie," she trilled. "Oh, and don't forget you're on playground duty first thing in the morning."

She smiled a knowing smile.

This wasn't how he'd planned his teaching career to go, but the All Saints' Junior School Christmas Nativity play had put paid to any hopes he'd rise rapidly through the ranks and manage to avoid minor irritations like playground duty.

And it would have worked too, if it hadn't been

for that stupid play and the headteacher's amorous advances.

Well, the *ex-headteacher's* amorous advances.

At least Miss Skate, or as the children had very aptly dubbed her *Mistake,* had abruptly left All Saints', taking all her unwelcome opinions on running a successful, politically-correct school with her – much to his relief and to that of the other members of staff.

Unfortunately, Ruth Abraham and Laetitia Gibbons, his colleagues, simply wouldn't believe that despite he and Mistake sharing a room at the Wickleston Arms on the evening of the Nativity Play, everything had been completely innocent.

But it *had* been completely innocent.

They'd both passed out after the landlady had liberally bestowed her powerful punch on all the patrons that evening, to make up for the fact that many of them were sheltering there because of the freezing fog. When they'd woken up in the morning, Mistake had apparently been feeling a little frisky but Oliver had hastily pulled his clothes on and left.

He felt particularly aggrieved because Ruth and Laetitia had almost forced him to offer the headteacher a lift and then pretend his car had broken down, to prevent her turning up at the Nativity Play and now, he was paying the price. And the price was that he had to do more than his fair share of playground duty.

He picked up his bag and went outside to the waiting cab. And that was another thing he had against Ruth and Laetitia – his car had never been the same since he'd pretended it had broken down; it was as if it was paying him back for casting aspersions on it when it was perfectly healthy.

"Bad day?" the driver asked as Oliver got into the passenger side of the cab.

Oliver nodded. He didn't want to talk. He'd spent hours today, talking to children, who, if their comments about cress and heart attacks were anything to go by, only half-listened.

"I'm Harris," the driver said, holding out his hand. "I'm new."

Oliver shook his hand. "Yes, I can see," he said. Cab drivers usually just drove. They didn't, as far as he knew, introduce themselves with a view to becoming life-long friends. Oliver looked at the identification card in front of him – Harris Tweed.

Harris saw the direction of his gaze. "Good, eh? Harris Tweed. Sounds really posh, don't it?"

Oliver agreed it did.

"You know what you need?" Harris said.

Oliver could think of plenty of things but he didn't want to discuss them with the driver.

"What you need," said Harris, "is some life-coaching."

Well, that hadn't been anywhere on Oliver's list.

"I do?"

"Yup, definitely. And it's your lucky day because I can offer you some."

Inwardly, Oliver groaned.

"Now let me guess," said Harris. "You're not happy in your career?"

"Well…"

"Say no more. I'll sort you out. Now, what d'you like doing? What's the most important thing to you?"

"I like to make a difference."

"Right, I've got the perfect job for you," said Harris after only a moment's thought.

"Yes?"

"Yep. Fork-lift truck driver. They make a difference. They move stuff from one place to another and make things look really different."

Oliver glanced sideways to see if Harris was joking but it appeared he was serious.

"I'm not terribly spatially aware, so I'm not sure that's quite suitable. And I was thinking more of making a difference to people's hearts and minds."

"Oh, I see. Well, how about a doctor, they dabble with hearts and minds?"

"I think there's quite a lot of training involved in becoming a doctor. I might've left it a bit late for that."

"Never say never, mate! If that's your dream, make it happen."

"Yes, but it's not my dream. I faint at the sight of blood. I was thinking more of helping people to be the best they can be."

"I've got it!" said Harris. "Cheese-maker."

"Why?" Oliver asked after a few moments.

"Everyone loves cheese. Lots of protein and calcium. Makes people strong – and happy."

"When I said 'the best they can be', I was thinking more of helping children develop and grow into useful, well-adjusted adults.

"I've got it!" said Harris. "Why don't you become a life-coach?"

"Well, to be honest, I'm not exactly sure what qualifications I'd need."

"No, me neither," said Harris.

"But I thought you said you were a life-coach."

"Me? Nah! I just said I could offer you some life-coaching. I'm an amateur. I throw my advice in for free with the cab ride."

"I see," said Oliver.

The cab drew up outside Oliver's flat.

"Here's one last bit of advice I'll throw in," said Harris as he turned the clock off. "Whatever you do, keep your chin up, put your best foot forward and don't let 'em grind you into the dirt."

"Thank you," said Oliver, looking through his wallet to find a five-pound note as a tip. He didn't usually give cab drivers that much but he felt Harris had been trying so hard, he deserved something extra. His own car was going to be delivered later, so hopefully, he wouldn't need a cab again. And if he did, he fervently hoped it wouldn't be driven by

Harris Tweed – he couldn't afford to spend so much on travelling to and from work.

But, *don't let 'em grind you into the dirt was good advice.* Tomorrow, Oliver would assert his rights. He'd done nothing wrong, so there was no reason why he should have to suffer playground duty more than anyone else. He'd get Alice Skipper to alter the rota. He couldn't believe he hadn't simply insisted on that in the beginning.

As he let himself into his flat, he was already planning next week's science club. It would be about keeping fit and healthy and he'd make sure to emphasise there was an important distinction between cholesterol and chlorophyll.

There was nothing wrong with teaching, he decided, nothing at all. And thanks to Harris Tweed's life-coaching, he now knew exactly what he wanted to do with his life.

The Hen Night

Persephone Perkins, CEO of *Persephone's Perfect Wedding Planning*, took the orange garment out of its bag and holding it by the shoulders, allowed the legs to dangle.

"What the heck is that?" Aunt Edie asked.

"It looks like she's holding up someone's shadow," Mary whispered with a shudder.

"I think it's an orange catsuit," Betty said, shaking her head in disbelief.

"I'd never get into *tha*t!" Florrie looked down at her ample hips, then back at the skinny costume the wedding planner was holding up.

"Of course, you will. Look..." Persephone pulled sideways and the catsuit stretched to several times its usual width. "I've got a range of sizes, from small to jumbo, so I'm sure I'll have one to fit everyone."

"That Lycra's certainly got a lot of give," Aunt Edie said, "but isn't it going to be a bit clingy?"

"It's a catsuit," said Persephone coolly. "How often do you see a baggy cat?"

"But it'll show all my bulges," Florrie said.

"I've thought of that," Persephone said looking Florrie up and down, "so I got bomber jackets to go over them." She pulled one out of the box and held it up in her other hand.

"And you expect us to wear those to Betty's Hen

Night?" Mary asked, shaking her head in disbelief. "They're both orange! They'll clash horribly with my hair."

"Don't worry," said Persephone, laying down the clothes and taking a small packet out of her box. She opened it to reveal a green beret. "You can tuck your hair into this."

Dipping into her box again, she withdrew a matching green, feather boa. "And here's the final part of the outfit."

"Couldn't we wear ordinary clothes?" Betty asked, a hint of desperation in her voice.

"Absolutely not!" said Persephone. "A successful Hen Night needs a theme."

"And what *is* the theme you're proposing?" Florrie asked. "Wearing those orange catsuits, it's going to look like we got trapped in a spray tan booth and have just escaped."

"I promise you," said Persephone, "these outfits will be the envy of everyone and you'll have the perfect Hen Night."

"But you said there was a theme," said Mary, "so, what *is* it?"

"Carrots," said Persephone.

There was silence while Betty the bride-to-be, Mary and Florrie her bridesmaids and Aunt Edie self-appointed chief guest, digested this information.

"Perhaps you'd care to elaborate…?" Betty asked eventually. After all, she was paying for Persephone's services even if the woman made it sound like she was doing Betty a favour.

"Well," said Persephone, fluffing up her blonde hair, obviously relishing the fact that all eyes were on her. "Firstly..." she said, leaning forward as if confiding an important secret, "what do you think of this? I've got you tickets to see the Eye-kia Boys."

More silence as the ladies looked at her in bewilderment.

"I thought you said the theme was carrots. You didn't mention furniture," said Betty. "Anyway, you don't need tickets to go to Ikea."

"No, not Ikea... *Eye-kia!*" said Persephone. "You know, the male troupe of dancers."

"You mean like the Chippendales?" Mary asked, her eyes wide in alarm and her cheeks reddening.

"Similar," said Persephone, "but the Chippendales are performing in Las Vegas this Saturday and they're much too expensive for Betty's budget."

"But, don't they..." Mary blushed, "err, don't they... strip down to their smalls?"

"If they're anything like the Chippendales, they won't be *smalls*," said Aunt Edie with a knowing nod.

"Aunt Edie!" said Betty. "How on earth do you know that?"

Aunt Edie winked. "I was young once, you know." She turned to Persephone. "Well, that still doesn't explain the carrots..." She gasped in horror, "does it? They don't do anything risqué with carrots, do they? Please tell me they don't!"

"No!" said Persephone. "Not as far as I know. The carrot theme is more to do with the second part of the evening."

"Second part?" Mary asked weakly. "You mean there's more?" her voice trembled.

"Of course!" said Persephone. "I've managed to get you into…" she paused dramatically, "The Khaki Carrot! The newest and fabbest Vegan Nightclub and Restaurant in Basilwade!"

"When you say *vegan*, do you mean, well… *vegan?*" Florrie asked. "Only I don't do fad diets."

"Veganism isn't a fad, I assure you," said Persephone. "It's the hottest new thing."

"Not if it's salad, it's not hot," said Aunt Edie. "I loathe salad. All that chewing! It's not dignified."

"Oh, I *see*," said Betty. "The Khaki Carrot. And that's why we're supposed to dress up like carrots?"

Persephone nodded with enthusiasm. She was almost hugging herself with glee.

"But," said Florrie, "why are the catsuits orange?"

Persephone shook her head and tutted as if dealing with a rather foolish child. "Because, my dear, carrots are orange."

"Don't you take that patronising tone with me, miss!" said Florrie, crossing her arms indignantly. "I know carrots are orange but you said we were going to the Khaki Carrot! So why didn't you bring camouflage catsuits?"

"Look," said Betty making calming gestures with her hands. The last thing she needed was for her wedding planner and her Maid-of-Honour to get into a fight, "let's calm down. We'll have a nice cuppa and then we'll talk the arrangements over some more."

"Non-refundable?" spluttered Florrie when Persephone explained she'd already purchased tickets and costumes. "You mean we've got to wear those ghastly clothes and go to watch men prance about in their undies and then eat cabbage?"

"You're going to love it! You'll have such fun!" Persephone said.

When the wedding planner had gone, Florrie held up her catsuit. "I suppose I could make dusters out of it," she said.

"Florrie! Betty's just paid for that! The least you could do is be grateful," said Mary.

"Yes, I suppose so. Well, in that case, perhaps we'd better try them on."

"That dreadful woman was right about one thing," said Aunt Edie. "We *have* had such fun, although I don't suppose she intended it to be because we were trying on those outfits! I've never laughed so much in my life." She flung the end of the feather boa over her shoulder with a flick, sending Mary into paroxysms of giggling.

"I'm not sure we look much like carrots though," Betty said wiping away the tears of laughter, "but you're right Aunt Edie, we have had fun, and to think, the Hen Night's not until Saturday!"

"Yes," said Mary, "but I'm pretty sure if we asked we might get our money back for the tickets."

"Although…" said Aunt Edie, "I rather enjoyed the Chippendales when I saw them… The Eye-kia Boys might be good."

"Aunt Edie!" said Betty.

"What? It's just a bit of innocent fun."

"Innocent?"

"Well, of course! It's always nice to see a well-dressed young male dancer."

"But I thought that was the point," said Betty. "I thought they weren't well-dressed."

"Oh yes," said Aunt Edie. "Beautifully dressed. You know, smart trousers, shiny shoes and bow ties."

"Well, perhaps we ought to go and find out," said Florrie. "It can't be that bad, surely?"

"And if we don't like it, or it's too embarrassing, we can leave, can't we?" said Mary, hope lighting her eyes.

On Saturday evening, the ladies assembled at Betty's house, ready to start the Hen Night. They'd arrived dressed in their own clothes along with their orange bomber jackets, green berets and feather boas. And just in case Persephone turned up to check, they took the precaution of hiding their catsuits in their handbags.

"I'm sorry, Betty," Mary said, "I just couldn't bring myself to put that catsuit on."

"Me neither," said Betty, "but I think we all look splendid in our own clothes. And the jackets, berets and boas are enough to give a nod to carrot-dom."

The bell rang and Betty opened the door.

"Good evening, ladies. I'm Harris Tweed, your chauffeur and life-coach. Miss Perkins hired me to convey you to your Hen Night. Your carriage awaits."

"Did that young man say we were going in a coach?" asked Aunt Edie. "Only I get sick in coaches."

"No, Aunt Edie, Persephone has laid on a car for us."

"D'you think he's bought a stretch limo?" Aunt Edie whispered.

"Knowing Persephone and her obsession with themes, it's likely to be a vegetable truck or a supermarket delivery van," said Florrie.

It was, in fact, an ordinary taxicab.

Betty, Aunt Edie and Florrie squeezed in the back and Mary blushed as she realised she'd have to sit in the front next to Harris.

"That's a very fetching hat, you're wearing, miss," he said to her and she blushed even harder.

"Th… thank you. I'm afraid my hair keeps falling

out of it," she said peering at herself in the vanity mirror on the visor and tucking stray curls up into the beret.

"Why don't you leave it?" he said. "I think all those red-gold curls look glorious."

"G… glorious?" Mary stammered and held her hands to her cheeks to hide her blushes.

"I always say redheads have such beautiful, milky skin with angel kisses all over their noses," Harris said.

"I should leave Mary alone, Harris," Florrie shouted from the back, "she gets awfully embarrassed and if her cheeks get much hotter, she's going to spontaneously combust."

Harris pulled up outside the Basilwade Theatre and rushed around to open Mary's door and help her out.

"Don't worry about us, we'll manage to struggle out of the car on our own," Aunt Edie grumbled as she climbed out.

"I hope you have a wonderful time, ladies," Harris said, "and I'll be here to pick you up when the show's over." He winked at Mary.

"I think Mr Tweed's taken a shine to you, Mary my girl," Aunt Edie said.

"Rubbish," said Mary with a furtive glance over her shoulder at the driver.

"I thought you said the men would be beautifully dressed, Aunt Edie," Betty said.

"They were!"

"But when you said they had bow ties, I assumed you meant they were wearing them on their shirts."

"I didn't mention shirts. Just bow ties. Weren't they magnificent?"

"But you definitely said they were wearing smart trousers."

"Well, they were – until they took them off."

"Their bodies were certainly very… um, dashing," said Mary.

"And so… *bulgy*," said Florrie. "I've never seen so much muscle, all rippling under lightly-oiled skin."

"Oh, stop it!" said Betty. "You're bringing me out in goose bumps!"

They were all laughing when they arrived back at their taxicab.

"Evenin' ladies," Harris said, holding the front passenger door open for Mary. "It sounds like you all had a wonderful time. Strap yourselves in – we're off to the Khaki Carrot."

The four ladies sat at the bar.

"Let's start with cocktails," said Betty, passing around the menus.

Aunt Edie studied the cocktail list. *"Cauli Wobble?* What's in that?"

Betty read out the ingredients, "Cauliflower florets, whiskey, vermouth, bitters and an olive."

"Hmm, I'm not sure I like the sound of that. What's in a Parsnip Paradise?"

"Parsnips, sherry, vodka, mango juice and an olive."

"These cocktails sound revolting," said Florrie.

"Well, it's one way of getting your five a day," said Betty. "Come on! Let's try something. I know the evening Persephone planned was a bit unusual but we've all enjoyed it so far, haven't we?"

"All right," said Florrie, "I'll have a Strawberry Salsify Sizzle, please – and don't tell me what's in it. I don't want to know."

The others decided on Cauli Wobbles and Betty gestured to the barmaid.

"Yes?" the large, well-built woman in a green apron said brusquely. "Vot can I get you?"

"Vilya? Vilya Chekarova?" Betty said, her mouth agape as she recognised the woman who'd been a personal trainer at Muscle Bounders Gym.

"Oh, it's you," Vilya said dismissively. She looked as if there was a disgusting smell beneath her nose. "Betty from the gym." She peered at the four women. "Vy are you all looking so stupid please? Are you pretending to be carrots? Those hats are ridiculous and vot is this?" she said holding Betty's boa up between finger and thumb.

"How dare you?" said Betty. "You rude woman. If you must know, these are guests at my Hen Night and next week, I'm going to marry Sydney Jugg, the man whose business idea you stole."

"Bah!" said Vilya, her hands on her hips. "Three course meal smoothies vere stupid anyway."

"That's not the point! Sydney could've made it work if you hadn't tried it and given several people food poisoning!"

"Vot rubbish!" Vilya said with a toss of her head, and then added, "So, you are marrying Syderney? You must be desperate!"

"I am not desperate! And it's *Sydney!* His name's *Sydney!*"

"That is vot I said – Syderney! Ha!" she said, her lip curled in contempt. "That man is a vimp!"

"How dare you call my fiancé a vimp!" Betty balled her fist and despite Vilya being almost twice her size, in height and width, she was poised to swing, ready to defend Sydney's honour.

Vilya opened her mouth to reply, then froze. She appeared to be focusing on something or someone behind Betty and the look of scorn was instantly replaced by a deferential expression. In a silky voice, she said, "Good evening, ladies! May I get you a drink? I recommend the Vortercress Virl or perhaps the Ginger and Shallot Shocker."

Startled at the sudden change in demeanour, Betty un-balled her fist and meekly took the drinks menu that Vilya proffered.

"Good evening," said a voice from behind them. It was a tall, smartly-dressed man with a badge on his lapel – *George Myers: Manager.*

"Firstly, ladies, may I say how marvellous your outfits are! So in keeping with our modest establishment," he said.

"Zey are supposed to be carrots," said Vilya, smiling proudly as if she was responsible for the jackets, berets and feather boas.

"Yes! Yes! I can see that! What a wonderful idea! Please order what you like, ladies – on the house!"

"Well, let's start with three Cauli Wobbles and a Strawberry Salsify Sizzle please," said Aunt Edie quickly. "You know, Mr Myers, this is my niece's Hen Night. I was wondering if perhaps you could see your way clear to giving us a meal on the house as well?"

"Aunt Edie!" said Betty, embarrassed at her aunt's audacity.

Mr Myers laughed and nodded. "Why not? You ladies have given me an excellent idea for staff uniforms. When we opened, we decided to go for green aprons, however, as you can see, they're not very distinctive. But I love your colour scheme and those jackets and accessories! They're simply marvellous! They'd look spectacular on our staff."

"And how about this?" Aunt Edie asked, taking her orange catsuit out of her handbag. "That lovely barmaid, Vilya, would look marvellous in this!"

"Aunt Edie!" Betty gasped.

"Yes," said Florrie, taking her catsuit out of her handbag. "See how much it stretches." She pulled it sideways. "I'm sure this would fit over all of Vilya's very substantial body. They'll fit anyone."

Mr Myers nodded approvingly. "And where can I get hold of these amazing garments?"

"I'm sure my fiancé, Sydney, could get you sufficient for all your staff," Betty said. "He's so entrepreneurial!"

"And in the meantime," said Mary, "why don't you take these samples?" she got hers out of her handbag.

"Thank you so much, ladies!"

Vilya returned with the drinks and placed one in front of each of the women.

Betty beamed at her friends. This Hen Night was turning out to be wonderful after all.

And then Aunt Edie made it even better.

"Here," she said giving Mr Myers her beret and boa, "why don't you ask our lovely barmaid to try out the whole ensemble now. I'm sure she'd love to, wouldn't you Vilya, dear?"

It had been just as well Persephone had booked Harris to take the ladies home. Vegan cocktails as served in the Khaki Carrot turned out to be more potent than the guests on the Hen Night had suspected – or perhaps Vilya had been more generous than usual with the alcohol. By the time they arrived at the Willows Retirement Home, it was locked for the night and Matron had not been happy about Aunt Edie's late arrival, nor about the song she was singing – nor the actions which went with it.

When they arrived at Florrie's house, she couldn't find her door key and Harris feared she'd left it in the Khaki Carrot and that he'd have to go back to retrieve it. But finally, after tipping the contents of her handbag over the doorstep, she found it.

He then took Betty home and watched her weave her way up the front path. She successfully negotiated the dustbin and the disgruntled cat to reach the front door, only to find she couldn't get the key in the lock. It was Harris who remembered he'd picked her up from the house next door and led her to the correct keyhole in the correct door.

The ladies had been so drunk, no one had noticed that although Florrie and Mary lived next door to each other, only Florrie had got out. So, once Harris had dropped off Betty, Mary was still in the car.

Rather than being annoyed, he was thrilled at having extra time with her.

What a beautiful creature she is, he thought.

"I think I'm going to be sick," Mary said as he helped her up the path to her door.

"Well, perhaps I ought to pop round tomorrow to see how you are," he said.

"That'sh very kind."

"All part of the service," Harris said.

The Stag Do

"What can we do which won't involve tying me to a lamppost, tattooing my face or relieving me of my trousers?" Sydney asked.

It was the planning meeting the week before the Stag Night and the bridegroom-to-be was sitting in the Petulant Partridge Tavern, next to his brother, Toby, who in two weeks' time, would be his best man. Across the table were the two ushers-to-be. Sydney's cousin, Derek Carruthers was one. The other was Sebastian Milligrew who Sydney had met for the first time that evening.

Betty's best friend, Florrie, had recruited Sebastian to be the second usher when it became clear Sydney didn't have many friends. And strangely, although Sydney's brother, Toby, maintained he came from a large family, Sydney claimed *he* didn't – sometimes, even denying he had a brother.

Sebastian belonged to Florrie's knitting group, *Blankets and Blarney,* and she'd persuaded him to be the usher at the wedding after Betty had confided in her that she feared her wedding was going to be lopsided.

"I've got so many friends and family and Sydney doesn't seem to have many people except his brother – and he doesn't like him very much. My side of the church is going to be full but Sydney's…"

Betty hadn't been able to finish and Florrie, who couldn't bear to see her so upset had resolved to try to fill Sydney's side of the church – somehow. She'd offered Sebastian free lifetime membership to *Blankets and Blarney* if he'd be the usher. In the end, she'd had to throw in some wool as well, in addition to promising to provide Hobnob biscuits at each meeting for the next year, before he'd agreed.

The bargain was struck and now, he was attending Sydney's pre-Stag Night planning meeting.

Each man slowly sipped his pint, deep in thought.

"Why didn't you get the wedding planner to organise your Stag Do?" Toby asked.

"Because she's bonkers, that's why," said Sydney.

The four men raised their pints to their lips and drank.

Eventually, Toby said, "I know a bloke what had pipe dancing at his Stag Night."

"What's that then?" Derek asked. "Is it like sword dancing?"

"Nah, it's girls swinging on pipes."

"What, like monkeys?"

"Nah. They hang on to the pipe and… sort of wiggle."

"I think you mean pole dancing," Sebastian said.

"Yeah, mebbe," Toby said, "poles, pipes. They're all the same."

"How about going Salsa dancing?" Sebastian said. "I belong to a club. It's good fun."

"Hoh! I was thinking of watching girls dancing, not doing it ourselves," said Toby. "What d'you think Syd?"

"I'm not sure Betty would like it if I spent an evening ogling at dancing girls a week before my wedding," Sydney said. "And don't call me Syd. You know I don't like it."

"It's better to watch them *before* you get married rather than after, Syd… *ney*," Toby said, ignoring his brother's look of annoyance.

"Girls dancing up poles could be considered an art form," Derek said. "You could tell Betty we were appreciating the arts…"

"You mean like ballet?" Sebastian asked.

Toby grimaced. "Nah, I was thinking more of the can-can or something a bit more… well… colourful."

"Colourful?" scoffed Sydney. "You don't know the meaning of the word! Only *you* could believe there's a colour called Mint Pink!"

"Mrs Harbottle loved it in her living room! You're just jealous because her husband praised my decorating and then didn't give you a bank loan. And I'm not surprised! Fancy wanting to manufacture aftershave what smelled of mackerel!"

"Bacon! It was bacon, not mackerel! Who on earth would wear aftershave smelling of fish?"

Sydney glared at Toby.

Toby glared at Sydney.

"You know, Ballet can be quite colourful and umm… interesting," said Sebastian soothingly, "and there are men as well as women, so no one could complain there's gender exploitation. I know of a lovely performance of *Swan Lake* where the roles are reversed."

"What! You mean all the dancers are replaced by swans?" Derek asked.

"Not species reversal!" Sebastian said. "I mean the roles that are usually taken by women, are taken by men and vice versa."

"Who wants to watch a load of geezers dance?" Toby asked.

"I'll have you know they're very good! I've seen it twice," Sebastian said.

"It doesn't matter," said Sydney. "I don't want to watch *anyone* dance."

"Well I know a lovely Salsa club, if you prefer—"

"You already told us about that and my brother said no," said Toby.

"I rather think it was you who said no." Sebastian tossed his head crossly.

"Chaps! Let's not fall out over Sydney's Stag Do!" Derek said, checking his watch. "If I'm going to catch my bus and get home at a reasonable time, we need to make our minds up quickly. So, how about… um…" he glanced around the dingy pub for inspiration and his eye rested on a poster, "the theatre! Yes, how about the theatre?"

"What's on?" Sydney asked.

Derek squinted at the faded sign and read, "*Macbeth*. There are no dancing girls in Macbeth, as far as I know. Not that I've seen the play. Or read the book. Although people always talk about breaking legs when Macbeth's mentioned, so I couldn't actually vouch for it not having any dancing. Perhaps there's a lot of dangerous stuff like tightrope-walking or people on stilts."

"That sounds more like the circus than Macbeth," Sebastian said.

"Circus! That's always fun. How about that?" Derek asked.

"There isn't one on next weekend."

"So, it's back to Macbeth, then?" Derek sighed and checked his watch.

"I think you'll find we're a bit late," said Sebastian.

"You can say that again!" Derek said crossly. "There are only two more buses before I'll have to walk home."

"No," said Sebastian. "I meant we're late because that poster's two years old."

"Well, what's on at the Basilwade Theatre next weekend?"

Sebastian consulted his phone. "The Eye-kia Boys."

"Is that Shakespeare?" Derek asked.

"Don't think so," said Toby. "It sounds more like a demonstration on how to put flatpack furniture together."

"It's a troupe of male dancers," said Sebastian. "They're very good. I've seen them."

"Dancers!" said Sydney, rolling his eyes to the ceiling. "What's the big deal about dancing? The whole world's gone dancing mad!"

"I guess it's because of Strictly," Sebastian said.

"Strictly what?" Derek asked.

"I don't care!" said Sydney. "I don't want to watch or take part in dancing. I don't even want to hear the word again! Is that clear?"

The four men stared into their pints as they sipped silently.

Derek checked his watch and drummed his fingers on the table top.

"I know!" Sebastian said, making the others jump. "I'll search on Google for Stag Night Ideas."

"Good plan!" said Derek. "I hope it won't take long."

"Here's a good website," said Sebastian. "Right, how about bungee jumping? Or white-water rafting?"

"In Basilwade?"

"Hmm, yes, I take your point."

"Can't we go to the pub?" Toby asked.

"You mean like we're doing now?" Sydney asked.

"Yes! We all love a pint. You'll enjoy it, Syd."

"It's not exactly a barrel of laughs this week, what makes you think it'll be more fun next week?"

"Well, all right, how about we go out for a meal?"

suggested Toby. "There's a new restaurant everyone's talking about which has just opened up in Basilwade."

"The Khaki Carrot?" Sebastian asked.

"Yes, that's the place. Is it any good?"

"Yes, if you like vegan food."

"Absolutely not!" Toby said once the others had explained what *vegan* meant. "If they don't do steak and chips, it's not a proper restaurant in my opinion."

"Go-karting?" suggested Sebastian.

"No," said Sydney.

"Darts Tournament?"

"No."

"Cave diving?"

"Don't be ridiculous!"

"Zombie Boot Camp?"

"No."

"Jelly wrestling?"

"What?"

Derek tapped his watch and stood up. "I'm sorry, chaps, I'm going to have to leave you to come to a decision about next week on your own. I've got a bus to catch…" He strode away before Sydney could stop him.

"I ought to be going too," Sebastian said, putting on his jacket.

"What? You can't leave until we've decided on

something!" Sydney said, jabbing the air with his finger. "You're my usher. So, ush!"

"I keep suggesting things but you don't want to do them," Sebastian said crossly. "I'm clean out of ideas."

"But can't you think of something ordinary? I mean to say! Jelly wrestling! I don't even know what that is! Why can't you come up with something I'd like to do?"

"Because I don't know you!" said Sebastian. "I don't know what you're interested in or anything about you!"

"He's not interested in anything, are you Syd?" said Toby.

"I am! And don't call me *Syd!*"

"Well, what *do* you like doing?" Sebastian asked.

"Umm… Oh you know! The usual things. Probably the same sort of things you're interested in," said Sydney.

"Well, I like doing the thing you said we weren't to mention and I also like knitting," said Sebastian.

"I don't think Syd can knit," said Toby, "and he definitely can't… you know…" he wiggled his hips as if dancing. "How he's going to do his first waltz with Betty at the reception, I don't know."

"My *what?*" asked Sydney his eyes wide with shock.

"Your first waltz. The bride and groom always dance first before everyone else joins in."

Sydney sagged backwards into his chair. "What! You mean with everyone watching?"

Toby and Sebastian nodded.

"Help!" wailed Sydney.

"That wasn't quite what I had in mind when you invited me," Toby said a week later at the Stag Night.

"Well, you pointed out you didn't want to dance," said Sydney, "and you didn't. Typical Toby! Wanting to please himself and not join in!"

"Oh, shut up, Syd! You were the one who said you didn't want to hear the word 'dance' mentioned again and then – blow me down, we spent the night dancin'!"

"*We? We? You* didn't dance, as I've already pointed out!"

"I wanted to watch girls dance. I didn't want to spend the evening watching you, Derek and Sebastian struttin' your stuff," Toby said.

"Well, that's your fault," said Sydney. "You could've joined in! You were just sulking because Miss Sanchez danced with me."

The brothers were glaring at each other, their shoulders tense and their fists clenched.

"More drinks?" asked Sebastian, eyeing the two men, fearful they'd fly at each other. But his suggestion was enough to remind Toby and Sydney they were in the Petulant Partridge Tavern and not at home. They relaxed and sank back into their seats.

"Allow me to get another round," said Sebastian chirpily, then as he stood to go to the bar, he added, "as usual," beneath his breath.

"Very good of you, old chap," said Derek. "Make mine a half, I've got to go shortly—"

"Yes," cut in Sebastian, "I expect you've got a bus to catch."

"Exactly! How did you know?" asked Derek.

"A lucky guess."

As Sebastian walked to the bar, he hoped that Derek, knowing his cousins' fierce rivalry, would steer the conversation away from the dancing lesson which they'd had that evening with Salsa teacher, Miss Sanchez, and find some safe topic which would ensure they finished the evening amicably.

"Miss Sanchez is a bit of all right, isn't she?" Derek said loudly. "At least you were able to watch her dance, Toby. I had to partner Sebastian."

"You all right, love?" the barmaid asked as Sebastian groaned and rolled his eyes.

"I will be next week, when the wedding's over," he said, "assuming the bridegroom doesn't murder the best man first – or vice versa."

But by the time he returned with the drinks, it appeared the trouble had been resolved as the three men were agreeing on the Salsa teacher's finer points.

"Hoh! Yes, Miss Sanchez is definitely a smooth mover," Toby said. "I expect it's all that Latin blood."

"And at least now, Sydney'll be able to dance the first waltz with Betty and not trample her to death," Derek said peering at his watch.

They sipped their beer in silence.

"Same again?" Toby asked.

The others nodded.

"Be a good geezer and get another round, Seb," Toby said checking his wallet. "I seem to be a bit short. I'll pay you back next week."

"Like you paid me this week for what you owed me last week?" Sebastian muttered to himself as he got up for another round.

"Just a—" Derek started.

"Half for you because you've got a bus to catch," Sebastian cut in.

"Yes, how'd you know?" Derek asked.

I'm going to see if Florrie'll provide cake each week at Blankets and Blarney. Sebastian thought. Hobnobs were all well and good but after the expense of this wedding, he was going to need carrot cake at least. And as for the emotional wear and tear…

When he arrived back at the table with the drinks, it appeared the alcohol they'd already drunk had begun to mellow the brothers and cousin who were reminiscing about old times.

Perhaps they will get through the wedding without a punch up, Sebastian thought.

"I wonder what Betty and her friends are doing

on their Hen Night, tonight?" Sydney mused. "I don't s'pose it was as exciting as our evening, eh?"

"I bet they just stayed home," said Toby. "You know what women are like."

"So, it's probably best if Betty doesn't find out about me dancing with the delectable Miss Sanchez or about us coming to the pub… eh? Probably best if we keep it to ourselves," Sydney said, a worried frown on his face. "I wouldn't want Betty to think badly of me."

At that moment, across town, Betty was in the Khaki Carrot sipping a Cauli Wobble cocktail with her friends and recalling with shrieks of laughter the moment when Florrie had tucked a fiver into one of the Eye-kia Boys' thongs…

The Perfect Wedding

Betty woke early the morning of the wedding.

At last, the day she'd longed for had arrived and the weather looked like it was going to be wonderful.

Everything would be perfect.

The rehearsal in All Saints' Church the previous evening had gone well although Betty made a mental note to ensure Sydney and Ichabod Bunch, who was going to be giving her away, were to be kept apart. They'd almost come to blows because Sydney hadn't liked it when Ichabod had taken her arm as he led her up the aisle.

"You don't need to maul her," Sydney had said and it had taken Reverend Forbes-Snell to calm him and explain Ichabod had behaved with propriety, in a way which would make Betty feel at ease.

"You wouldn't want her to feel nervous, or indeed to trip, would you, Mr Jugg?"

And Sydney had assured the vicar he wouldn't.

Betty, still lying in bed, ran through the entire service in her mind and then got up and showered. Florrie and Mary would arrive soon ready for their makeover. Persephone had booked someone who would make the bride and bridesmaids look 'simply divine'. And shortly after, Ollie, her nephew would come and take the first of the wedding photos.

Betty was impressed when the make-up artist who Persephone had described as having a 'magical touch' arrived a few minutes before nine o'clock. At least she was punctual.

"Morning," she said in a singsong voice when Betty opened the front door. "I'm Bella Carrossetti from Bella's Beauty Box – Beauty in Basilwade or Wherever You Are. I believe your daughter's expecting me."

"My daughter?" Betty asked in surprise.

"Yes," Bella peered at her from beneath heavy, false eyelashes. "Aren't you the bride's mother?"

"No! I'm the bride!"

"Oh, thank goodness for that!" Bella's thick but perfectly-shaped eyebrows drew together. "I haven't allowed enough time to make up anyone who's not on my list today. Right, lead the way. I've got another wedding to do at midday."

Betty took her to the bedroom where Mary and Florrie were waiting. They both blanched and stiffened when they saw Bella.

"This is Bella," Betty said.

"Yes, we've already met." Florrie threw Mary a meaningful glance.

"Oh yes, I remember you ladies! You ran that knitting club that closed down, didn't you?" she said to Florrie.

"Florrie still runs a knitting club. It hasn't closed down," said Betty.

"Yes, it has!" Florrie and Mary said together.

But Bella was engrossed in taking her makeup and brushes out of the box and arranging them on the dressing table.

"Who wants to be first?" she asked scrutinising each face in turn. "I usually do the one who'll take less work first but you all look like you're going to need my maximum attention."

"What a rude and tactless woman!" Betty said as soon as Bella had gone.

"I know," said Florrie. "She came to one of our *Knit and Natter* sessions in the community hall. That's why it closed and reopened as *Blankets and Blarney* in my house."

"Still," said Mary, peering into the dressing table mirror, "she knows her stuff. She's actually made my hair look quite nice and the concealer she applied has covered most of my freckles."

Florrie and Betty gazed into the mirror, turning their heads to view themselves from all sides and both nodded with satisfaction.

"Well, shall we get dressed?" asked Betty. "Harris'll be here with the car soon, to pick us up."

Florrie and Betty were too absorbed in their own reflections to notice Mary's blushes which, whilst muted somewhat by the layers of concealer, still flared brightly, causing her complexion to go a deeper shade of pink than her dress.

"I'll go!" Mary said when the doorbell rang. She grabbed the voluminous skirts, ran downstairs and threw open the door.

"Oh!" she said in disappointment.

"Hello, I'm Oliver Primm. I've come to take Auntie Betty's wedding photos. Is everyone decent?"

"Ah, Ollie!" said Betty from the landing. "Come on up, we're ready."

As Oliver galloped upstairs, Mary poked her head around the front door and scanned the empty street. It was much too early for Harris to be there but a girl could hope. With a sigh, she closed the door and went upstairs for the 'Primping Photos' as Betty had called them.

Mary shot downstairs when the bell rang a second time, only to find Persephone and her young son, Ulysses, dressed in a miniature suit with a top hat under his arm.

The young boy scowled at her, as if daring her to agree with his mother that he was the height of cuteness and that Betty was going to adore him.

"I had no idea he'd look so delectable in top hat and tails," Persephone said. "I'm thinking of renting him out at the weekends for people's weddings."

From the boy's sulky expression, Mary suspected that was unlikely to happen.

She'd got to the top of the stairs with the wedding planner and page boy when the doorbell rang again and pointing the way to Betty's bedroom, she grabbed her skirts and rushed downstairs. Surely this time it would be Harris…

It wasn't. It was Brenda Baskin with the bride's

bouquet and bridesmaid's posies which Mary took into the kitchen. She'd just finished standing them in jugs to keep them upright when the doorbell rang again.

It was Ichabod Bunch, dressed in a smart suit, top hat and the capacious, black cape he wore during his shows.

Mary showed him into the front room and made him tea, then after a sneak peek out of the front window to see if Harris had arrived, she went back upstairs.

When Harris finally knocked, Ichabod Bunch beat Mary to the door.

"You look beautiful. A real dream," Harris said as he helped Mary out of the car when they arrived at the church.

"Stop it!" said Florrie. "If you keep making her flush like that, the heat'll melt her makeup and it'll all slither off."

Betty had other things to worry about. "Is he here?" she asked anxiously. "Has Sydney arrived yet?"

"I'll go and have a look," said Harris and as he hurried up the path to the church, Mary watched him with adoration in her eyes.

"What d'you reckon about those two, Ichabod?" Florrie whispered. "Is there another wedding on the cards?"

"There's always another wedding on the cards, dear lady," said Ichabod in an otherworldly voice.

"Oooh!" said Florrie, staring into his eyes.

Harris came out of the church and gave the thumbs up sign to Betty, who'd been holding her breath. She sagged with relief. Getting married hadn't been Sydney's priority and she'd had to nudge him a bit to get him to propose. Suppose now the big day had come, he'd changed his mind? He could be quite stubborn when he set his mind to it. So, Harris's signal lifted a great weight.

"Shall we?" Ichabod tossed the cape over one shoulder and offering Betty his arm, they walked up the path, followed by Florrie and Mary in their pink dresses, then Ulysses with his hat tucked under his arm, out of which, peeped Wormwoman. Oliver stood to one side, taking photos and Persephone was next to him, hands clasped together – although whether in rapture or supplication, it wasn't clear.

"Mum?" Ulysses said pointing to the edge of the churchyard. "Did you order a turkey?"

From behind a large, stone tomb, strutted an enormous bird which appeared to be dragging something behind it. Catching sight of the bridal party, the bird raised its iridescent tail feathers fanning them in an elaborate display and shaking them as if quivering with delight.

"Persephone!" said Betty, her eyes nearly popping out of their sockets. "How marvellous!

Where on earth did you hire a peacock? Oh, you wonderful woman!"

"I… I…" said Persephone, staring at the bird. Then gathering herself, she added, "Oh you know…"

As if on cue, the peacock joined the end of the line and followed the bridal procession up the path to the church.

Ichabod opened the door slightly and peeped in to signal to the organist, Mr Sykes, the bride was ready and that he could begin the Bridal Chorus, when Mrs Myers, the churchwarden, rushed over.

"We're not quite ready," she whispered.

"It's Sydney, isn't it?" Betty squealed. "He's changed his mind, hasn't he?"

"Not as far as I know," Mrs Myers said looking over her shoulder at the bridegroom and best man waiting at the altar. "It's the vicar."

"He's changed *his* mind?" Betty asked. "Is he allowed to do that?"

"No," said Mrs Myers, "of course he hasn't changed his mind about performing the ceremony! He's just lost his reading glasses, that's all. He's gone back to the vicarage to try to find them. Probably just as well or he'll end up reading the wrong words and performing a baptism or burial. But don't worry, he shouldn't be long."

Betty put her eye to the gap and peered through. Sydney was indeed at the front with Toby, both of them looking very smart in their top hats and tails.

"Can you see Sebastian?" Florrie asked.

"No. I can't see Derek either," said Betty.

"Thank goodness for that!" said Mary. "That man's a monster."

"Here, let me look, Betty," said Florrie. "You'll mess your headdress up and you don't want to be seen before your grand entrance."

They swapped places and Florrie opened the door wider.

Mrs Myers appeared again. "Don't worry," she whispered. "Reverend Forbes-Snell won't be long."

"We were wondering where the ushers were," Florrie said, "only we were worried the church would be lopsided with the bride's family all on one side and only a few of the groom's family on the other."

"It looks fairly even to me," said Mrs Myers. "I'll go and see the ushers."

Sebastian appeared at the door a few seconds later.

"Well done!" Florrie said. "Where did you manage to get so many people for Sydney's side of the church?"

"We did the 'knit one, purl one' method of seat arrangement," said Sebastian.

"What's that?"

"Sent the first group to the bride's side and the next to the groom's and so on."

"But they're all muddled!"

Sebastian shrugged. "So what? Most of them

didn't seem to know each other anyway. You were worried about it being wonky – and now it's not."

"Well, yes, I suppose so."

"Anyway, I've got to go, I'm teaching Derek how to knit. He's already checking his watch. If I don't keep his mind off the time passing, he'll be outside at the bus stop."

"What's going on?" Betty asked. "Is it all going horribly wrong?"

"No, not at all," said Florrie, "other than the vicar being late, it all seems to be perfect."

"Mrs McSquirtle! Mrs McSquirtle! Where are you? I can't find my reading glasses!" Wilbur Forbes-Snell yelled as loudly as he could. "Dratted woman!" he muttered under his breath. "Oh, Hettie, why did you desert us?"

"Are you callin', Reverend?" Mrs McSquirtle said coming out of the kitchen with the tea towel as if he'd caught her in the middle of drying up dishes. She had in fact been searching for the key to the cocktail cabinet where the vicar had taken to hiding the brandy.

"Yes, Mrs McSquirtle! It's an emergency! I have a couple waiting for me to perform their wedding ceremony and I can't find my reading glasses. You don't know where I left them, do you?"

Mrs McSquirtle placed her hands over her apron pocket, inside which the glasses lay hidden and pretended to consider. "Hmm. They could be anywhere. The last time you lost them they were locked in your desk."

"Were they? I don't remember that!" Wilbur took the keys from his pocket.

"Although," said Mrs McSquirtle you might have left them in the bathroom. Give me the keys and I'll see. You look upstairs. It's most likely they're in your bedroom."

"I'll check my desk, you go upstairs."

"I would, Reverend, it's just my shrapnel wound," she said holding her foot out and wiggling it.

"Oh, all right!" Wilbur said, handing over the bunch and with his robes gathered in one hand, he took the stairs two at a time.

Mrs McSquirtle was in the dining room before the vicar had reached the top step and she'd opened the cocktail cabinet, removed two bottles of brandy, locked the door and hidden the bottles under the table.

Then, returning to the hall, she shouted up the stairs, "I've found them, Reverend!" And taking the glasses case from her apron pocket, she placed it on the palm of her hand.

"Bless you, Mrs McSquirtle! What would I do without you? I won't need dinner, by the way, I'll be at the reception in the church hall," he said as he took them and rushed back to the church.

Mrs McSquirtle removed the cocktail cabinet key from the ring and put the bunch on the vicar's desk in his study.

Then returning to the cocktail cabinet, she helped herself to a glass of 'medicinal' gin and taking the two bottles of brandy from under the table, she went back in the kitchen and hid them under the sink.

She'd forgotten about the wedding. Oh well, there was no point cooking for one – not that she had much in the house anyway and if it was a large wedding, there was bound to be plenty of spare food. She might just wander over later and see if they needed a hand. It wouldn't be the first time she'd joined the end of a queue for the buffet at a reception in the church hall. But first, she'd have a fortifying glass of 'medicinal' brandy.

Wilbur dashed across the churchyard, his robes flapping, and he arrived at the altar red-cheeked and out of breath.

"So sorry! I do apologise!" he gasped. "Is the bride here?"

Sydney nodded and looked fearfully over his shoulder.

"If you're havin' second thoughts, now's the time to scarper," Toby said.

"As best man, you're supposed support the groom," said Wilbur, his lips pressed angrily together.

"I am, mate. Trust me, I am supporting him. I've been down the aisle three times and wished I'd scarpered before I got to this bit."

Sydney's breath came in short, sharp bursts and his eyes swivelled as if looking for escape.

"Although, havin' said that," continued Toby, "if I *had* scarpered, those women would've hunted me down and killed me." He placed his hand on Sydney's shoulder. "Yes, you've let it get this far, so it's probably best if you carry on."

"Sydney?" Wilbur pinned him with a hard stare.

Sydney swallowed and nodded.

"Like a lamb to the slaughter," Toby whispered cheerfully.

Wilbur cleared his throat and peered over the top of his reading glasses to Mrs Myers at the far end of the church who was waiting to open the door. She nodded, then looked at Mr Sykes seated at the organ with his hands poised over the keyboard, ready to play. She nodded pointedly at him. Then as she stepped forward to open the door, the organ began and familiar notes drifted out into the echoing church. The guests fell silent as everyone swung round to see the bride and her party.

"Oooh! Doesn't Betty look beautiful?" said Aunt Edie to the other members of the Willows Retirement Home who Matron had delivered earlier that day in the minibus. She'd not been happy about letting them out of the home but the wedding invitations had seemed genuine. Before she'd let them go, she'd insisted on searching them for spades, shovels or any other digging implements.

"We're goin' to a weddin', not a do-it-yerself funeral!" Len had complained. "Why would we want spades?"

"I don't trust you near a graveyard," Matron said.

"You were wrong the last time when you thought we were digging up the dead," said Myrtle, "and you're wrong now. We went down to Slee-on-Sea to go sailing, not grave-robbing."

"Oh, don't think I'm not looking for sailing equipment at the same time as I'm searching for spades," Matron said.

"We're just going to Betty's weddin'!" Len said. "I don't know why you have to make everythin' into a drama, Matron."

"It's not me making things into a drama, Len Malone. And I don't want any of your blue comedy routine performed at the reception! Is that clear?"

"Yes, Matron!" Len said with a salute.

"Glory be! Is that my Mary?" Mrs Wilson exclaimed, pushing her spectacles further up her nose. "I've never seen her look so nice." She nudged the man next to her and pointed out her daughter. "Are you still single? I'll introduce you after, if you like," she said.

"Aah! Look at the funny little page boy!" Myrtle said to Dora. "Have you ever seen such a scowl on a small boy?"

"What's that following the page boy?" Dora asked.

"It looks like a peacock," said Len.

"Isn't it amazing what they can do with animals these days?" Dora said.

"Why, what've they done to it?" Dora asked.

"Trained it, of course."

"Is it real?" Myrtle asked.

"Of course, it's real," Dora said, "…Isn't it?"

"I wonder if it'll raise its fan?" Len asked, prodding the feathers with his foot as it passed.

The peacock turned its head, fixed Len with a beady eye, then throwing its head back, it screamed, "Oh-ow! Oh-ow!"

The piercing shrieks soared towards the ceiling, bringing the organ music to an abrupt halt.

For a moment there was silence which was broken only by Charlie Chubb's high-pitched giggle coming from the vestry where Mrs Myers insisted he remain during services.

As if in answer to Charlie's laughter, the peacock opened its beak wide and shrieked again.

"What's going on? Is someone hurt?" Wilbur asked, craning his neck to see around the bridal party who were proceeding up the aisle.

"It's a peacock," Len shouted back although his voice was drowned by the, "Oh-ow! Oh-ow! Oh-ow!" sound which bounced off the walls, then collided with the echoes that reverberated in the rafters. Guests looked around in confusion.

"Somebody get that thing out of here before it deafens us!" Mrs Myers shouted, climbing on a chair with a hymn book in either hand, ready to bat it away should it turn round and go for her.

From the organ loft, Mr Sykes was unable to see what was causing the racket and he stood, enraged that anyone or anything should interrupt his musical flow. He scanned the pews for the noisy offender who was disturbing him, then spotting the peacock, he held up his hands in horror.

"Get that creature out! I'm allergic to birds. Oh, my hands! My hands!" he sobbed although no one heard over the shrieks of the enraged creature.

"Somebody do something!" Wilbur yelled, grabbing his robes ready to flee should the peacock get as far as the altar.

It was Ulysses who took the initiative by dropping his top hat over the bird's head. True this did little to calm the peacock which screamed even louder and thrashed about frantically but it muffled the sound slightly and the fact that it could no longer see gave Len the confidence to pick it up, tuck it under his arm like a set of bagpipes and rush outside. With one hand, he whipped off the top hat and with the other, he propelled the peacock away from the church – but not before it had pecked his finger, drawing blood.

Len swore loudly. Then crossed himself three times.

He hurried into the church, slammed the door and made his way back to the pew, to the applause of the congregation.

"That was very brave," said Myrtle.

He sank down on to the pew and held up his hand to show her the peck wound.

"Matron's never going to believe I was attacked by a peacock," he said gloomily. "She'll probably say it's the Mark of the Beast."

"Don't worry," said Myrtle, "the photographer got the entire thing on video."

Wilbur cleared his throat loudly and pointedly.

The congregation fell silent.

Charlie Chubb continued to giggle hysterically, having disobeyed Mrs Myers orders and opened the vestry door a crack to see what was going on.

Mr Sykes sobbed quietly as his hands swelled up like sausages.

"Dearly beloved..." began Wilbur.

Oliver Primm was beginning to despair. It was one thing taking photos of the bride and her bridesmaids while they posed in his aunt's bedroom and quite another attempting to capture the formal family groupings outside the church – which is what most people expected from their wedding photos. Keeping a class of thirty six-year-olds under control was simple in comparison to positioning the guests in a pleasing and well-balanced arrangement at his aunt's wedding.

It was like herding ants. As soon as he took his eyes off anyone, they moved.

And the hats! So many large, elaborate creations which concealed smaller guests with their lace, feathers and flowers.

As soon as he'd arranged everyone in an attractive

grouping where he could see all faces, someone announced they were off to the toilet.

The only person who didn't seem reluctant to be in his photos was a small, barrel-shaped woman dressed in black who he didn't recognise. She shouldered her way to the front on several of the shots where she smiled, posed and winked for the camera. It was refreshing to find someone who obviously enjoyed being photographed and Oliver, assuming she was a well-loved relative, asked Betty if she'd like him to take a photo of the two of them.

Betty professed not to know the woman and it was only when Reverend Forbes-Snell caught sight of the small woman who was posing like an Egyptian sand dancer in front of the group, it appeared she wasn't a guest at all.

"Mrs McSquirtle! What are you doing?" the vicar had shouted, to which she'd yelled "Peacock!" and pointed towards the wooded area at the edge of the churchyard. In the ensuing chaos, small, plump Mrs McSquirtle had disappeared and it had taken Oliver some time to convince everyone she'd been mistaken about the reappearance of the bird and to get them back into order again. Even worse, he'd hurt his back helping several of Aunt Edie's friends off the table top tomb which they'd somehow managed to scramble on to, in their efforts to escape the peacock.

He quickly flicked through the photos he'd taken on his camera, mentally ticking them off the list.

Bride and Groom.

Bride, groom, best man and bridesmaids.

Bride and bridesmaids.

There were a few where he'd have to do a bit of judicious cropping and remove the groom from one of the pictures with photo-editing software. Betty wouldn't want a reminder of the incident which almost turned into a punch up between Sydney and the esoteric gentleman in the cloak.

Thankfully, he seemed to have sufficient photos. And it was just as well because most of the guests had lost interest and were now wandering towards the church hall for the reception.

"Wipe that sour look off your face, Sydney!" Betty whispered to her new husband as he glared at Ichabod who was making a speech.

"...And, finally, I'd like to toast the newlyweds. I predict much happiness and joy." He raised his glass. "Let's drink to Mr and Mrs Jugg."

"Mr and Mrs Jugg!"

"You'll note he didn't say he predicted *we'd* have much happiness and joy. He just said he was predicting there *would be* much happiness and joy. Charlatans like him never come out with anything specific. It's all sweeping generalisations," Sydney said to Betty.

"Oh, Sydney, don't be such a crosspatch! You're so suspicious! Ichabod was being pleasant. Now, please be nice," she said as her husband rose to give his speech.

He stuttered and stumbled his way through his thanks and with a nervous look at Toby he sank back into his seat. Public speaking definitely wasn't his thing but he knew his brother was more confident than he had a right to be, and guessed Toby wasn't daunted by the thought of giving a speech. He also suspected he was about to be ridiculed. And if the number of pages Toby was unfolding was anything to go by, his humiliation was going to be prolonged and profound.

Entries in his Book of Grievances were also going to be prolonged and profound although he'd probably put off doing them until tomorrow. He was sure Betty wouldn't let him sit up tonight writing until he'd finished recording everything.

And there was still the indignity of the first waltz to be endured. After that, there wouldn't be much more to suffer – the wedding would practically be over. Thankfully.

But in the meantime, he was at Toby's mercy and there was nothing he could do about it except smile and wait for him to finish.

"...Hold a grudge? Let me tell you, my brother, Sydney's, won medals for grudge-holding..."

The guests laughed.

"Yes," Toby continued, "I remember when Syd was three—"

"Shpeech!" shouted Mrs McSquirtle banging the handle of her knife against the table and holding up her glass of champagne.

"I'm *doin'* a speech," said Toby crossly.

"Rightio! Well, now the shpeeches are done, letsh have cake!" she shouted, then fell over sideways.

"Mrs McSquirtle!" said Wilbur, rising from his seat, spotting her scrambling to her feet at the far end of the table and glaring at her. "What on earth are you doing here? Have you been drinking? You can't simply turn up at a wedding uninvited!"

Sydney saw his opportunity to shut Toby up and he grabbed it. "Don't worry, Reverend, she *has* been invited."

"Has she?" whispered Betty. "Who is she?"

"She's my… err… cousin. A distant cousin," said Sydney loudly, "and she's got the right idea, let's cut the cake!"

"I didn't know she was our cousin! And I 'aven't finished my speech!" said Toby.

Sydney shrugged, raising his hands in a gesture of helplessness. "Oh dear. Never mind. Now, who wants cake?"

The guests cheered.

"Right, let them eat cake!" said Sydney cheerfully, grabbing Betty's hand and leading her to the three-tiered chocolate gateau.

Oliver took a series of photos of the bride and groom, starting with their hands on the large, silver knife with its tip poised over the chocolate icing, and finally, the blade buried to its hilt. As he checked each one, he noticed the small, round woman, who was apparently Sydney's distant cousin somewhere in the photo behind the newlyweds. *More photo-editing*, he thought with a sigh although perhaps he'd leave her in the photos. She added a bit of interest, especially when she struck that Egyptian sand dancer pose although her attempt at crowd surfing had fallen rather flat.

Literally.

It appeared that lying horizontally whilst being passed from hand to hand over the heads of a crowd wasn't a concept most of the guests at the wedding were acquainted with and when the small, rotund woman had swallow-dived onto a group of them, they'd not been prepared. Or perhaps she hadn't been crowd-surfing at all. Some said she'd simply climbed up the DJ's stack of speakers and had toppled off. Luckily, no one had been hurt.

As soon as the food had been cleared away, the dancing had started, beginning with Betty and Sydney's waltz. Oliver made sure he had plenty of shots of that and then his colleagues, Laetitia Gibbons and Ruth Abraham, had led the line dancing. He'd not forgiven them for that embarrassing evening he'd spent with headteacher, Miss Skate but he had to admit, for old dears, Laetitia and Ruth were pretty nimble on their feet and he made sure he had a range of photos of them with the guests trying hard to follow the steps.

And then, just as his camera battery was about to run out, the bride and groom thanked everyone for coming and the evening wound up.

He was packing away his camera, when that nice usher, Sebastian, had suggested they meet up for a drink in the Petulant Partridge the following week.

Now, to go home and download everything off his camera.

"So, if this marriage doesn't work out, can I get my money back?" Sydney asked as they sat at their kitchen table after the reception.

"What!" Betty spluttered, spilling her tea.

"Only joking!"

"I should hope so too, Sydney Jugg!"

He smiled at her and patted her hand. "You know, Mrs Jugg, that wasn't such a bad day, was it?"

She returned his smile. "It certainly had its moments!"

"I know! I hope that wretched wedding planner doesn't charge you for the peacock! Although it was rather entertaining! Especially when Len Malone tucked it under his arm and ran outside with it like he was playing rugby although I thought Matron was a bit harsh when she came to pick the residents up."

"There was no need for her to frisk all the Willows residents before she let them on the minibus."

"It's a shame those two old people got locked in the broom cupboard," said Sydney. "It's lucky they didn't have heart attacks, getting stuck in a confined space at their age. I wonder how it happened?"

"Oh, don't worry about Dora and Rex, they're used to it. They spend a lot of time in broom cupboards."

"Why? Are they obsessed with cleanliness?"

"I wouldn't say so," said Betty, "it's more of a… erm hobby." She quickly changed the subject. "Wasn't it nice that Mary and the chauffeur seemed to be getting on. Mrs Wilson was overjoyed. She cornered the churchwarden and provisionally booked All Saints' for a wedding next April. But it's best we don't tell Mary that."

"My cousin, Derek, and Florrie seemed to be getting on well too. He was still at the reception chatting to her, long after the last bus had gone."

"Your other cousin, Mrs McSquirtle's, a character. I can't believe you've never mentioned her before. She's quite a livewire."

"Hmm," said Sydney vaguely.

"I wonder where the peacock went. Someone said it was only calling out like that because it was looking for its mate. I hope he finally found her," she said squeezing Sydney's hand.

"I expect he did. Basilwade's not a very large place."

"Mmm. Not very large, no. But I love living here.

It's a friendly town, isn't it? People meet people and become friends and then through them, they find more friends until they're all friends together..."

Sydney tipped his head to one side as if considering the matter.

"I mean," continued Betty, "it's like Basilwade is a place where a giant hand dropped a bag of magnetic balls."

Sydney considered this in silence for a moment. "Is it?" he asked, finally.

"Yes."

"How?"

"Well, the balls would roll all over the place but gradually, they'd join up into pairs and then into small groups until the whole lot was stuck together in one lump."

Sydney considered again.

He tried his best, imagining magnetic balls rolling through the streets of Basilwade but it was no good, he didn't have a clue what Betty was talking about. And anyway, if magnetic balls had been in a bag, wouldn't they all be stuck together? When the giant hand dropped them over the town centre, wouldn't they simply have caused a crater? Obviously not in the world Betty was imagining.

"Jolly good," he said finally, hoping that Betty would be satisfied with that. *This*, he told himself, *is the mysterious nature of marriage.* There would probably be lots of times in the future when life would become unfathomable and he'd just have to find strategies to cope. Perhaps diversionary tactics would work.

"So, are you going to make a full English breakfast tomorrow, Mrs Jugg?" he asked wearing what he hoped was his most winning smile.

About the Author

Dawn's first success was with a short horror story published in a charity anthology entitled *Shrouded by Darkness* in 2006.

Several years later, she had a Young Adult book *(Daffodil and the Thin Place)* and a single author anthology of speculative fiction stories *(Extraordinary)*, published as well as several historical romances, set mainly during and between the two world wars.

She has written two plays about the First World War, one of which commemorated the beginning of the war and was first performed in England in 2014 and then in France and Germany. The other play commemorated the end of the war and was performed in England in 2018 and in Germany 2019.

Using her World War One research, she has also written a book entitled *The Great War – One Hundred Stories of One Hundred Words Honouring Those Who Lived and Died One Hundred Years Ago.*

Other Writing by Dawn Knox

Extraordinary

Published by Bridge House

From the furthest reaches of the universe, to the inside of a cardboard box, assorted characters play deadly games with their victims while others play practical jokes on angels or dirty tricks on aliens. Some have good intentions, others are scoundrels and a few are truly evil – but all of them are EXTRAORDINARY.

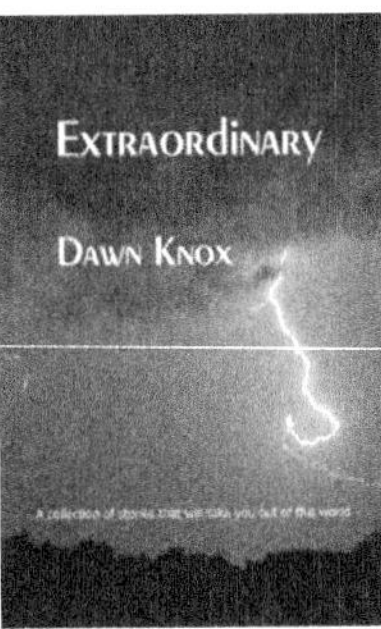

"A wonderful collection of amazing stories. An enjoyable read."
(*Amazon*)

Order from Amazon:

Paperback: ISBN 978-1-907335-51-8
eBook: ISBN 978-1-907335-52-5

The Great War

Published by CreateSpace

100 stories of 100 words honouring those who lived and died 100 years ago.

"I love this book. What an interesting and 'novel' way to write about so many different people's experiences. I have dipped in and out, back and forth a number of times. It certainly lends itself to re-reading. Highly recommended." (*Amazon*)

Order from Amazon:

Paperback: ISBN 978-1-532961-59-5
eBook: ASIN B01FFRN7FW

Welcome to Plotlands

Published by Ulverscroft

1930: Joanna Marshall lives with her beloved mother in the household of her somewhat less-beloved aunt, who wishes the pair of them gone. When her mother dies, a grief-stricken Joanna sees an opportunity to escape – Ma's title deed to a rural patch of land. Welcomed into the Plotlands community, Joanna begins to make a new life for herself, and meets handsome solicitor Ben Richardson. But he wouldn't be interested in an ordinary girl like her… would he?

A Touch of the Exotic

Published by Ulverscroft

From India to war-torn London to an estate in Essex, Samira's life is one of rootlessness and unpredictability. With her half-Indian heritage, wherever she goes she's seen as 'exotic', never quite fitting in despite her best efforts. To add to her troubles, her beauty attracts attention from men that she's not sure how to handle. But when she falls for handsome RAF pilot Luke, none of her charms seem to work, as it appears his heart is already bestowed elsewhere…

Order from Amazon:

Paperback: ISBN 978-1-444840-65-0

“The Best of CaféLit” series

Printed in Great Britain
by Amazon